CALIFORNIA TRAIL DISCOVERED

California Trail Discovered
Copyright © 2020
Marie Sontag, PhD

ISBN: 978-1-952474-31-6

Cover design by Farhan Harits.
Map design by Libby B. Hall.

Published by WordCrafts Press
Cody, Wyoming 82414
www.wordcrafts.net

CALIFORNIA TRAIL DISCOVERED

Book 1 of the Whitcomb Discoveries

MARIE SONTAG

WordCrafts Press

DEDICATION

California Trail Discovered is dedicated to my sister, son, daughter-in-law, and friends from California who, before I completed this book, flew out to Texas to be with me after a total of six surgeries nearly took my life. Many thanks to Laura Longshore, Jon and Rachel Sontag, Martha Stott, Sharon Ulstad, Linda Wells, and Mary Jane York. You showered me with true friendship and love.

Also, thanks for the love and amazing support shown to me during that time from my Texas son and daughter-in-law, Daniel and Meredith Sontag, along with my Texas friends such as Lisa Brand, Karen and Randy Gray, Julie Marx, Laura and Gary Pool, and Carol and Bob Wood.

Most of all, thanks to my husband and forever-friend, Mark. Your selfless servant heart always amazes and sustains me.

AUTHOR'S NOTE

As a former middle school and high school teacher, my teaching mantra has always been, "It's a sin to bore a student." I sought to make my lessons fun and interesting, hoping to impart students with a love for life-long learning. Now, as an author of middle grade and young adult historical fiction, I strive to do the same. My first writing aim is to entertain. My second goal is to share with readers facts previously unknown that can spark their interest and create a thirst to know more.

To that end, *California Trail Discovered* brings to light unknown facts about the historical figure of Jim Savage who, in 1846, traveled West on the same wagon train as the Donner Party. The story brings to light reasons why the Donner Party found themselves trapped in the Sierra snows while the fictional character of Daniel Whitcomb and the historical figure of Jim Savage did not.

After each chapter, I've included S.T.E.A.M. (science, technology, engineering, art, and mathematics) lessons classroom teachers and homeschooling parents can use along with this book, should they choose to include it as part of their curriculum.

Book 2 of this series, *Yosemite Trail Discovered* (a young adult historical fiction novel), follows Daniel, now 17, as he works with Jim Savage in the California goldfields. In 1851, Jim and Daniel fight alongside the members of the Mariposa Battalion and become some of the first whites to "discover" Yosemite Valley.

Oregon Country Territory
Unorganized Territory
Iowa Territory
Wisconsin Territory
Sierra Nevada Mountains
Fort Hall
Independence Rock
Fort Laramie
Princeton Township IL
Sutter's Fort
Chimney Rock
Fort Bridger
Platte River
Independence MO
Yerba Buena (San Francisco)
N
Mexico
Key
Oregon Trail
CA Trail
Greenwood Cutoff
Hastings Cutoff

1

THE FIRE

February 10, 1846
Princeton Township, Bureau County, Illinois

Daniel flailed his arms and struggled to free himself from Morgan's grasp. He stared at his childhood home, now engulfed in flames as he fought to pry Morgan's arms from around his broad chest. "Let me go!" His voice cracked. "Ma! Pa!"

A charred beam crashed down. The center of the roof caved in.

Daniel sobbed.

Pounding on Morgan's arms, he tried to wriggle free, but his father's business partner held fast. Daniel's breath came in short gasps as a chain of neighbors passed water buckets up the hill from the creek behind his house. Splashing buckets of water onto the flames did as much good as spitting on a garden to make it grow during a drought.

A full moon cast ghoulish shadows onto the ground. Reddish-orange flames licked the sides of the house and billowed out the roof. *I should've gotten here sooner.* Numbness rose from Daniel's feet to his arms. His whole body shook.

"I went to our blacksmith shop after supper…" Daniel tried to explain, but a wave of shock and hysteria cut off his thoughts. "Oh, God!" His voice cracked again.

Releasing his grip around Daniel's chest, Morgan laid a hand on the boy's shoulder—gentle, but firm.

Daniel turned to face him. "What am I gonna do?"

For a moment, Morgan said nothing. Then, as if waking from a bad dream, Morgan's eyes went wide. "Daniel, where's Hannah? Was she inside with your parents?"

Daniel glanced back at his skeleton of a house. Another beam crashed to the floor, causing sparks to fly. "No. Thank goodness. Hannah spent the night at Pastor Lovejoy's for Marybeth's birthday."

The fire continued to pop and whine as it consumed more of the house. Smoke curled upward, blotting out the stars. "What am I gonna tell Hannah?" He fought back the tears that mounted with each blink. "What'll I tell her about Ma and Pa?"

A week after the house fire, Daniel sifted through the scorched remains of his home in search of something to salvage. Kicking his parents' twisted metal bed frame, he glanced at Pastor Lovejoy. "Pastor, do Hannah and I have to move West with Morgan and his relatives?"

Pastor Lovejoy nudged a pile of ash with the toe of his leather boot. "Morgan's your legal guardian now. You have to go where he goes."

Daniel thrust his arm out and pointed west. "But all the way to the Oregon Country?"

The pastor pinned Daniel with a stare. "Son, it's your job now to care for little Hannah. You might only be thirteen, but you're a survivor. And, by God's grace, I know you'll do more than just survive. I believe the Lord's got important work for you to do."

Daniel swallowed the growing ball of fear lodged in his throat. *Important work? I doubt it. I'll probably end up disappointing Pa, just like always.* "Why did Pa pick Morgan as our guardian? He's not even married. Why didn't he pick Morgan's older brother, Jim?"

The large, middle-aged pastor pursed his lips and stroked his thick, brown beard. "Jim's a bit of a free spirit. As you know, he doesn't even attend church. On the other hand, Morgan's a god-fearing soul. Besides, with Morgan as your guardian, you can continue your apprenticeship as a blacksmith."

Daniel arched a brow. "Sure. Going to church is important. But at least Jim's married. Hannah needs a ma as well as a pa. Can't we just come live with you?"

A smile crept across the pastor's face. "Mrs. Lovejoy and I would be glad to have you and Hannah come live with us." He rubbed the back of his neck. "But I'm afraid you'd be in the same danger you were in when you lived with your parents."

"Danger?" Daniel dropped the half-melted fork and spoon he'd stopped to examine. "What danger?"

The pastor winced. "Remember how, the day after the fire, Sheriff Peterson found your parents' bodies in the ashes?"

Daniel trembled like he had the night of the fire. "Yes. They're at the undertaker's now until the funeral on Sunday."

"Well, Sheriff Peterson found evidence the fire wasn't an accident."

Not an accident? Daniel's breath caught in his throat. "What kind of evidence?"

"He found three empty whiskey bottles. One was near the front of the house, and two were in the back. The sheriff thinks alcohol was used to speed up the fire."

"Who'd want to kill my parents?" Bile rose to his mouth. He stepped away from the mounds of ash and plunked down beneath a leafless elm. Letting his head drop to his hands, he spoke as if talking to the ground. "What kind of an evil person would do such a thing?"

Silence hung between them.

Kicking at the pebbles and dead leaves beneath his feet, Daniel heard a clink. He brushed aside the debris and uncovered an empty bottle labeled Old Overholt. "Oh, God. Here's another one." With shaking hands, he stood and handed it to the pastor. "I swear, if I find out who did this, I'll kill 'em myself."

Pastor Lovejoy inclined his head. "Daniel, If you seek justice on your own terms, the anger will eat you up until there's nothing left of you. And, as I said, with Hannah only ten and her blind eye and all, you've got to think about caring for her now."

A pressure built up in Daniel's chest like when he swam in the creek and stayed underwater too long. "But why would anyone want to kill my parents? Everybody loved them."

The pastor paused and looked up at the gray, cloud-covered sky. "Remember last month when you woke up and came downstairs to find your pa and me giving a family some food and clothing? You asked why I was at your house so late."

Daniel pinched his bushy brows together. "I remember. But you didn't explain. You just said a free Negro family needed help, and you and Pa were helping them."

"Well, they weren't free Negroes."

Daniel studied the pastor's face. "You mean they were runaway slaves?"

Pastor Lovejoy nodded.

"So you think people who don't want slaves to go free set our house on fire?"

"I do." The pastor's voice took on a conspiratorial tone. "I know Judge Filbrush is good friends with a few southern plantation owners. Many southerners aren't too happy about their 'property' escaping through Illinois on their way to Canada. Did I ever tell you about my abolitionist brother, Elijah?"

Daniel shook his head no.

"Like your parents and me, Elijah believed slavery was evil. He printed a newspaper that said slavery should be against the law in all states. He was killed several years ago when an angry mob burned down the warehouse where he kept his printing press. Even though our state doesn't allow people to buy and sell slaves, it's still against the law to help them. Many people in Illinois think it's okay for people to own slaves."

Daniel studied the clouds that parted just enough to let through a thin ray of sunshine. *So that's what Pa was doing late at night when he thought Hannah and I were sleeping.* He couldn't imagine Pa breaking the law by helping slaves. It seemed there was a lot he didn't know about his father. He searched his memory for a clue.

"Come to think of it," Daniel said, "I do recall an argument Pa had last month with Mr. Flannery, the saloon keeper."

Pastor Lovejoy continued to search the ground for salvageable debris. "What was it about?" the pastor asked without looking up.

"One morning while Morgan was busy showing me how to repair a wagon axle, Mr. Flannery came by and asked if Morgan had time to fix a harness. Pa said Morgan was busy, but he would do it. The saloon keeper called Pa a few mean names and said he didn't want him touching his property."

Daniel paused his story when Pastor Lovejoy bent down and picked up a book with singed pages.

Daniel pointed at it, relieved to focus on something else besides his parents' deaths. "That's my Timothy Flint book about Daniel Boone. I loved that book."

Pastor Lovejoy handed the charred remains to Daniel. "You and a lot of other young people. I'm not sure how many of the stories are true, but I've heard it makes for adventurous reading."

Trying to inject some humor into the conversation, Daniel shot the pastor a wry smile. "What? You mean you don't believe Daniel Boone fought hand to paw with a bear? Or escaped from Indians by swinging on vines?"

The pastor chuckled. "No, I can't say as I do." He stroked his beard. "So, you are aware of at least two men in town, Flannery and Judge Filbrush, who were not very fond of your father. And I can think of a few others."

Daniel continued to search the ashes for other items to rescue. A few feet away he spotted the dirty remains of his stepsister's favorite doll. *Sweet Sassafras would want me to save this.*

He picked up the doll and smiled as he thought of his special name for Hannah. His stepmother often used sassafras tea to calm Hannah's reoccurring cough. He had adopted Sassafras as his pet name for her.

At ten, Hannah still enjoyed playing with the remains of her one-armed cotton doll. As hard as the past week had been for him, he knew losing their parents had affected her even more. Hannah hadn't said a word since she'd heard about their parents' deaths.

As he carried the doll down to the creek to wash off the grime, he thought about the first time Hannah stopped speaking. Hannah's mother told them it happened when Hannah's father died. He was a trapper, and they lived in a cabin far from civilization. Hannah was only three. They never would have survived if the friendly Ho-Chunk Indians hadn't taken them in.

After living with the Indians for two years, the tribe's medicine man said Hannah and her ma had to leave when Hannah's right eye began to wander. He said she had an evil spirit and that's why she had a strange eye and couldn't talk. Several from the tribe helped them make the journey through the Wisconsin Territory to Illinois. Daniel still remembered the first day he heard Hannah speak. It was only a few months after Hannah's ma and his pa married. But, now, after learning of her mother and stepfather's deaths, she'd stopped speaking again.

Reaching the creek, Daniel doused the doll in the cool, swift current. *God, I thought you were supposed to be fair and just. Doesn't seem like Hannah has seen much of that in her life.*

He rubbed away the smudges on the doll's face and pushed it under again. *I thought life was supposed to be fair. Ma and Pa always put others first. God, how could you let someone get away with murdering them?*

He tried to stand as he wrung out the doll, but his stomach wrenched. He leaned over to push out the pain. Everyone expected him to stay strong. How could he when the center of his chest had been ripped out, leaving only a large hole in its place? His eyes burned. Someday, he'd return to Illinois and find out who killed his parents. For now, he'd try to ignore the pain. The pain of losing his parents. The pain of losing his home. The pain of not seeing his pa and stepmother's killers brought to justice.

Straightening to his full height, Daniel stumbled back toward the ashen remains of his home. Focusing on the future made it hard to suck in a breath. Come spring, he and Hannah would travel for six months on a wagon train with Morgan and his relatives. They could die from Indian attacks, illness, bad weather, an accident, or lack of food. What if the stress was too much for Hannah? He gritted his teeth. Seems Pa didn't think about what might happen to his family if he helped runaway slaves.

He shook his head and considered Pastor Lovejoy's words. *Son, you're a survivor. It's your job now to care for little Hannah. And I believe the Lord's got important work for you to do.*

Daniel wasn't so sure about having important work to do for the Lord. But he swore he'd do all he could to protect them both. Whatever the cost.

S.T.E.A.M.

S.T.E.A.M. lessons to accompany California Trail Discovered can be found at:
https://www.mariesontag.com/resources/teacher/

While reading chapters 1-6, readers create a model of a covered wagon using the Engineering Design Process. Begin with the #5 *California Trail Discovered* S.T.E.A.M. Projects link, A_STEAM Intro.pdf

2

ON THE TRAIL

June 4–5, 1846
Colonel Russell's Wagon Train on the Great Plains
Unorganized Territory

Standing to the left of the oxen pulling their wagon, Daniel shouted, "Haw." Using his guide stick, he tapped the nearest ox on the rump, just as Morgan had taught him. The team veered left. He'd never traveled more than ten miles from home. Now, he and Hannah were walking across the Great Plains on their way to the Oregon Country.

For the past year, Daniel had worked in Princeton Township as a blacksmith apprentice under Morgan Savage's guidance. He had expected Morgan to continue the apprenticeship on the trail. He didn't. And, since his parents' deaths in February, Morgan had served as Daniel and Hannah's guardian. But, since joining Colonel Russell's wagon train in Missouri a month ago, Morgan hadn't been much of a guardian either. It made Daniel's blood boil. At first, he and Morgan took turns driving the covered

10

wagon he and Hannah shared with him. Lately, however, Morgan spent most of his time with Miss Frances Brisbin.

Miss Brisbin, along with her brothers and widowed father, also traveled with the wagon train to the Oregon Country. It seemed Morgan thought it was more important to help Miss Brisbin with the wagons owned by her family than it was to help him with the one he and Hannah shared with Morgan. Even in their spare time after supper, Morgan visited the Brisbins instead of continuing Daniel's blacksmith apprenticeship.

Morgan's older brother, Jim, took notice. Whenever they had a spare moment, Jim taught Daniel how to shoot. At first, he hesitated to accept Jim's offer. Pa had never shown him how to handle a rifle.

"It's good to have blacksmith skills," Jim said, "but now that you're a pioneer, learning how to shoot is more important."

For the past several weeks, Jim had taught him how to shoot glass bottles and pieces of wood. Today, Jim took him out to hunt buffalo.

Having ridden with Jim two hours ahead of the wagons, they now stood about fifty feet downwind from a massive herd of bison. Two of Jim's cousins, Peter and Charles, joined them in the hunt but had ridden farther ahead.

"If you can pick off one of the buffalos from here," Jim said, "we can field dress it before the wagon train catches up with us."

Daniel stared down the barrel of Jim's .50-caliber Hawken rifle, then paused to glance back at Jim.

"Focus on his ear," Jim reminded him. "Once you've got that in your sites, aim two inches lower, then two inches behind it. It's a hard shot, but if you can hit 'em there, he'll drop like a one-ton safe from twenty floors up."

"Wouldn't it be easier to just aim for the buffalo's lungs?"

"You could." Jim flashed Daniel a one-sided smile. "But the beast won't die right away. He'll leave a trail of blood you can follow. Eventually, the poor critter will drop, but he'll suffer till he does. You're right, though. The lungs are easier to hit than the brain. It's your choice."

Daniel put on a relaxed face but trembled with excitement as he pressed the rifle's butt to his shoulder. As Jim had taught him, he lined up his sights and squeezed the trigger.

Blam!

The rifle's recoil and deafening blast almost threw him off balance, but he held his stance. The three-quarter-ton animal gave out a short, pitiful bawl. As Jim predicted, the bullet to the beast's brain caused it to drop dead in a cloud of dust.

Daniel let out a whoop.

"Fine shootin', boy." Jim slapped him on the back. "You're a natural."

He inhaled. His chest swelled. Pa had always been short on compliments. *If Pa could only see me now.*

Trailing behind Jim, Daniel rode out to the buffalo and looped his reins around the animal's horns. Jim pulled out his Bowie knife, slit the bison down the belly, and showed Daniel how to skin it.

Jim's cousins must have heard the shot because they soon joined them at the side of the animal. "You work on skinning him," Jim told his cousins, "while I cut out its organs."

Jim showed Daniel how to cut the sinews that attached the buffalo's muscles to its bones. "The women can dry these and weave 'em together. The sinews make a mighty fine rope when twisted around each other. A man can never have too much rope."

Daniel turned his head to the side. He clutched the red kerchief around his neck to cover his nose, then stopped. He didn't want Jim to know how much the animal's stench made him gag. He wasn't sure if the musky odor came from the bison's matted fur, its thickening blood, or the meat and organs Jim had removed, but, having just gained Jim's respect, he didn't want to lose it. He tried to ignore the smell as he cut out strands of sinew. "How'd you learn to do all this?"

Jim carved out a slab of meat and transferred it to the canvas they'd laid on the ground. "I learned a lot from trappers when they came to town."

Peter laughed. "What our cousin's not telling you is that, when he was little, every time he went to town he'd visit the Food & Supply store to see if any trappers had come in to trade their furs. If they had, he'd beg 'em to spill their yarns 'bout life in the wild."

Charles nodded. "That's right. And then, when he was sixteen, Jim left home and became a trapper himself. He hunted, trapped, and occasionally lived with the Injuns. I think he got along better with them than he did his own folk."

Daniel let his jaw drop. "You lived with Indians? How'd you communicate?"

Jim nodded. "We used our hands a lot."

"He's being modest." Peter hacked another section of

the buffalo's hide. "Truth be told, Jim's got a knack for learnin' languages. He picks 'em up natural as a toddler learns to talk. Got to where he could speak the language of several tribes."

"So why'd you quit trapping?" Daniel asked.

Jim sawed away another sinew. "For one thing, beaver hats went out of style. And though I loved livin' in the wilderness, I eventually came back to marry Eliza."

"And look at him now." Charles swatted Jim's shoulder. "He's a respectable husband, soon to have one of his own little critters!"

Studying Jim, Daniel expected to see the silly grin of a soon-to-be father. Instead, Jim's face strained as he paused every few seconds to glance at the plains.

Daniel's muscles tensed. "Do you think Indians might attack us for killing this buffalo?"

Jim's gaze met Daniel's. "Early this morning we passed a mound of rocks near a grove of willows. Did you see it?"

Daniel shook his head. "No."

"It was a Lakota burial ground. The Lakota dress up their dead in fine clothes." Jim gestured with the tip of his bloody knife. "Then they wrap 'em up in buffalo hides and lay the corpses on long-poled platforms. Kinda like the ones I saw in the grove this mornin'."

Daniel stared down at the buffalo. "Guess I gotta pay more attention to what's going on around me."

"If you expect to survive out here, you do." Jim attacked another section of buffalo meat. "I've heard tell that the Lakota haven't really pestered any wagon trains passin' through here, but as more of us head west, I bet it'll stir 'em up pretty good."

Jim paused to survey the plains once more, then turned his gaze back to Daniel. "Out here, you've gotta be ready for anything."

When the wagon train caught up with the hunters, Colonel Russell brought it to a halt. "We'll stop here for a bite to eat," Russell shouted down the line.

No one disagreed.

Since Daniel, Hannah, and Morgan's relatives had joined Colonel Russell's wagon train in Missouri four weeks ago, more travelers had joined the group. The company had now grown to seventy-two wagons. The most recent pioneers hailed from the Springfield area and included the families, friends, and acquaintances of George Donner and James Reed, as well as an eye doctor, George Arnold, and his wife, Caroline. While the men in the group unhitched their oxen to let them graze, the women prepared the afternoon meal.

Before sitting down to eat, Mr. Reed and Dr. Arnold strode up to Jim and Daniel and complimented them on a successful hunt.

Eyeing the buffalo skin fastened behind Daniel's saddle, Reed whistled. "That buffalo fur will make someone a warm blanket. And I'll wager you'll get quite a few meals out of the meat."

Daniel nodded. "Meals and jerky."

Two German immigrants who had recently joined the wagon train, Lewis Keseberg and Augustus Spitzer, approached the group. Both Germans had buffalo robes draped over their shoulders.

"Ach, there is a much easier way to get a buffalo hide than to cut it off the animal," Keseberg announced.

"Ach, ya." Spitzer nodded. "Let someone else cut it off for you!"

The two men laughed.

Daniel glanced at Jim.

The man's hands curled into fists.

Before Jim took a step, Reed turned to face the Germans. "Gentlemen, where did you get those robes?"

Keseberg glared at Reed. "They were a gift."

Reed stepped closer to Keseberg and pointed his finger at the man's chest. "You don't say. A gift, huh?"

The large German slowly pushed Reed's hand away. "Do not all you Americans say, *the best Indyun is a dead Indyun?* This fur was a gift from a dead Indyun."

Daniel took an instant dislike to Keseberg. He clenched his teeth. He thought about the Ho-Chunk who had taken care of Hannah and his stepmother for three years. "No. Not all Americans say that," Daniel blurted out.

Dr. Arnold laid a hand on Daniel's shoulder as if to hold him back.

"Mr. Keseberg." Reed's pitch rose. His face reddened. "If you stole those buffalo robes from the Lakota Indians' burial ground, you must return them immediately."

Keseberg stood up to his full six-foot height and ran his fingers through his blond, collar-length hair. "The Indyun was dead. He will not need it to keep warm."

"You idiot!" Reed yelled. Before Daniel could blink, Reed slammed his fist into Keseberg's jaw.

Keseberg reeled but remained upright. He rubbed his chin and lunged toward Reed.

Jim whipped his handgun from his waistband and raised it above his head.

Blam!

"Enough!" Jim yelled.

Daniel's ears rang from the blast. The rotten-egg smell of gunpowder pricked his nose.

"This isn't open to discussion." Jim stared at the Germans. "If the Lakota come after us because you stole those robes, they'll take our scalps and kidnap our women and children. Return them at once!"

Keseberg eyed Jim's pistol. If the man's eyes could shoot daggers, they'd all been dead.

"And just to make sure you get there safely," Jim said as he returned his pistol to his waistband, "I'll ride back with you."

Keseberg mumbled something in German and turned to retrieve his horse. Spitzer trailed behind him.

Jim watched the men head toward their horses. "It's men like Keseberg that'll get us all killed."

Mr. Reed massaged his knuckles. "I don't like resorting to violence, but, for some, it's the only language they understand." Reed turned to Daniel. "I hear you and your guardian are saddlers. One of my saddles needs attention. Can I bring it over later this evening? I'll pay you a good price for the repair."

Daniel nodded. "Yes, sir." He welcomed any opportunity to earn a little extra money. He'd need all he could get it if he ever expected to return to Illinois.

After Jim and the Germans returned from taking back the buffalo robes, the caravan continued on its way. Daniel drove their wagon's oxen as Hannah walked by his side. Morgan, as usual, spent the rest of the day helping Miss Brisbin's father drive their wagon.

Hannah hadn't spoken since they left Illinois. Maybe if she made friends with other girls on the wagon train, it would help. Personally, he'd rather spend time with books than friends. Besides. Taking care of Hannah, the oxen, and their wagon gave him more than enough to keep busy.

That evening Daniel prepared a cooking fire for Jim's wife while Hannah helped with the meal. When Jim, Morgan, and their cousins arrived for supper, Morgan let them know he wouldn't be joining them.

"Been invited to sup with the Brisbins. Just came by to wash and change my shirt."

Crossing his arms, Daniel glared at Morgan. "I was hoping you'd help me repair Mr. Reed's saddle while we still have daylight. Tried to fix it myself, but I need help."

Morgan washed his face and hands in the bowl of water Eliza had set out. "Give it another try, son." He dried his hands on the towel next to the bowl. "I'll look at it in the morning before we head out."

Daniel grabbed Morgan's arm. "How will I ever learn how to be a blacksmith and a saddler if you're never around?"

With widened eyes, Hannah covered her ears.

It pricked Daniel's heart to upset her, but now that he'd uncorked his rage, he couldn't keep it from spilling out. "You're supposed to be my guardian. Why don't you act like it? You should've left us in Illinois." Daniel released Morgan's arm and stomped out of the campsite.

"Come back here, son!" Morgan yelled.

Daniel didn't glance back. "I'm not your son."

"Let him go," Jim said.

Even Hannah's sniffles didn't stop him from walking out beyond the circle of wagons.

19

S.T.E.A.M.

Continue with Wagon Project at:
https://www.mariesontag.com/resources/teacher/

$$3$$

THE GREAT PLAINS

June 6–16, 1846
Colonel Russell's Wagon Train on the Great Plains
Unorganized Territory

Over the next week and a half, the scenery of the Nebras-kan plains changed little as the wagons followed the sandy borders of the Platte River. Clumps of trees occasionally broke up the wavy sea of emerald green grass while wild tulips, primroses, lupines, and larkspur presented a dazzling palette of color.

Although it had been four months since Daniel's parents' deaths, Hannah still hadn't spoken. Usually, she walked next to him as he guided the oxen that pulled the wagon they shared with Morgan. Today, however, Hannah picked wildflowers with Mr. Reed's twelve-year-old stepdaughter Virginia, and Virginia's younger sister Patty. Daniel smiled at the thought of Hannah making new friends.

"Oh!" Virginia's voice raised its pitch. "Look at those blue lupines. Let's be sure to pick some of those."

Hannah silently picked a few of the blue-spired

blossoms and added them to the flowers she'd gathered in her apron.

"And don't forget to watch out for buffalo chips." Virginia glanced at the metal pail she carried at her side. "We haven't gotten very many today."

Daniel saw Hannah's face pucker as if she'd sipped sour milk.

"I know it's awful to touch dried buffalo poo," Virginia said. "But we need it for the evening fires since there aren't many trees out here on the plains."

On some days, Virginia rode her pony alongside her father when Colonel Russell asked Mr. Reed to scout ahead for a suitable campsite for the evening. Daniel spent his days either hunting with Jim or guiding their wagon's team of oxen.

Occasionally, when Morgan wasn't spending time with Miss Brisbin or when Morgan asked one of his relatives to drive Daniel's wagon, Hannah would tug his hand and gaze at him with her baby blue eyes. She'd point at Virginia and Patty gathering flowers and buffalo chips, and pout if he didn't agree to join her as she walked alongside them. He usually gave in.

One evening after Daniel had pulled their wagon into position around the pioneers' camp, Virginia invited him and Hannah to join her family for a meal. "We're havin' biscuits, venison stew, and dandelion greens sautéed in butter," she said.

Daniel had never tasted venison stew or dandelion greens. He wasn't sure if he was up to trying new foods, but when Hannah batted her eyes at him and steepled her fingers as if in prayer, he reluctantly agreed.

As they neared the Reed's campfire, Mr. Reed invited them to sit on two overturned metal buckets. The younger Reed children, James Jr., and Thomas, sat on the back of the Reed's wagon. Virginia and Patty sat on large rocks near the cookstove while Mrs. Reed dished out the stew.

Virginia and Patty kept giggling and glancing Daniel's way. Like the warm flames of the fire, a wave of heat rose from his chest to his throat. The last thing he wanted was to have giggling girls as friends. *I've got enough on my mind caring for Hannah and driving our wagon.*

As Daniel shoveled in his last bite of stew, Patty pointed at Hannah. "Why does your sister have funny looking eyes?"

He hated answering that question. Since Hannah wasn't talking yet, it was up to him to speak for her. Daniel looked at Hannah for approval, and she nodded yes.

After taking a deep breath, he slowly exhaled. "Her eyes look a little different because the right one isn't centered. It's a little to the left. It's been that way since she was five. She doesn't see at all out of that right eye."

"How did it happen?" Virginia asked.

"We don't know why or how it happened, but I can tell you a story about *when* it happened if you'd like."

"Oh, please do." Virginia's eyes widened. "If that's all right with Hannah."

Hannah nodded.

"Okay." Daniel leaned closer to the fire. "As Hannah's mother explained to us, the story starts back when Hannah was only three, and her father, as usual, went deep into the woods to trap beaver."

"You don't have the same mother and father?" Patty interrupted.

"No." He shook his head. "Hannah's my stepsister. Her ma and my Pa got married four years ago when Hannah was six and I was nine. But, as I was saying, Hannah's father spent a lot of time trapping beaver deep in the woods. Then, one time, he was gone for over eight weeks. That's when Hannah first stopped talking."

Daniel picked up a stick and poked the fire, causing sparks to fly up. "Hannah's mother knew something must have happened to her husband. He'd never been gone that long. She didn't know what to do. She couldn't leave Hannah alone, but she also couldn't take Hannah with her to go and search for him. That's when the Ho-Chunk Indians visited their cabin."

Five-year-old James Jr. spoke up. "Were they good Indians or bad Indians?"

"Good Indians." Daniel poked the crackling fire once more. "The Ho-Chunks told Hannah's mother they'd discovered the remains of her husband's body far from the cabin. A bear had attacked him. They knew it was Hannah's father because the Ho-Chunk had given him a bear-tooth necklace that he always wore around his neck. Hannah and her mother lived too far from civilization to try and reach the nearest town by themselves, so the Indians convinced Hannah and her mother to live with them.

"They stayed with the Ho-Chunk for the next two years. Then, when she was five, her right eye stopped tracking with her left eye, and she gradually lost sight in her right eye."

Mrs. Reed, seated next to Hannah, reached over and patted her head. "Oh, you poor dear."

Pursing her lips, Hannah looked up at Mrs. Reed and nodded, as if thanking the woman for her concern.

Daniel continued. "The tribe got a new shaman when Hannah's eye started wandering inward and he said—"

"What's a shaman?" Patty tilted her head to one side.

"He's kind of a spiritual leader." Daniel rubbed his chin. "Sometimes the Indians call him a medicine man. Anyway, the shaman told the tribe that Hannah's wandering right eye would bring the tribe bad luck. He forced the tribe to take Hannah and her mother to the whites. The closest town was Princeton Township. It took them four days, but the Ho-Chunk made sure Hannah and her mother got there safely."

Mrs. Reed smiled. "And that's when your father met Hannah's mother and married her?"

Daniel nodded. "Eventually. Hannah's mother found work taking in people's laundry. My own ma died when I was four. In order to save money, Pa always washed his own clothes. But when his blacksmith business improved, he started taking our laundry to Hannah's mother."

James Jr. jumped up from his seat on the back of the wagon. "Four. That's about how old Virginia was when her papa died, right, Mama?"

"No, dear." Mrs. Reed lifted James Jr. off the wagon and settled him on her lap. "Virginia was only two when her father died. But let's let Daniel finish his story."

Shifting his position on the upended pail, Daniel continued. "When Pa married Hannah's ma, he also adopted Hannah. Two months after she and her mother became part of our family, Hannah started to speak again. We hoped her eye would also return to normal, but it didn't.

For the next four years, we all lived together as a family…
until our parents were killed in the fire. That's when
Hannah stopped speaking again."

Mrs. Reed wagged her head. "Yes. You poor dears. We
heard about that fire. Such an awful thing. Like flooding
after a severe storm, tragedy seems to hit every family at
some point or another."

Daniel's throat tightened. "I think what happened to
my parents was more than a tragedy," he spat out. "I think
someone intentionally set fire to our home. I've pledged
to go back someday and get to the bottom of it. When I
find out who—"

From somewhere nearby a fiddler struck up a tune,
interrupting their conversation. Virginia turned to Mrs.
Reed. "Oh, Mother, can we go and listen to the fiddler?"

Mrs. Reed laughed. "I'd say, after that sad tale, we could
all use some happy music. Virginia, why don't you, Daniel,
and Hannah find the fiddler. We'll come along after we
clean up."

Daniel was glad for the interruption. He grabbed Hannah's
hand and took off in the direction of the music. Children
cheered as they played tag around their campfires. Men
chatted about the next day's travel, and women described
the homes they'd establish at the end of the journey.

*That's what I need to do. Set my mind on the future, not the
past*, Daniel decided.

Finally, they found the campfire where a teenaged fiddler scratched out several familiar tunes, including *Old
Dan Tucker* and *Possum in a Gum Stump*.

In the dim light of the campfire, Daniel surveyed the
small crowd. His eyes paused on the lanky form of a young

man leaning against a wagon wheel near the fiddler. He knew him from somewhere. Then, like emerging from the fog of a bad dream, it came to him. The young man was Matthew Brody. Four years older than Daniel, Matthew had also lived in Princeton Township. Daniel searched the crowd for Matthew's younger brother, Josiah. He spotted him at the back of the group. The sight of the Brody brothers made Daniel's stomach twist. He recalled how the boys had bullied younger kids in the town's one-room schoolhouse until the teacher banned them from school.

Daniel turned to Virginia. "Let's go back to your family's camp." He squeezed Hannah's hand.

"But we just got here." Virginia rubbed a strand of her long blonde hair between her thumb and forefinger and sat on a boulder near the fire.

The fiddler struck up a lively rendition of *Buffalo Gals.*

Daniel pinched his lower lip between his teeth. "I know some of these boys from my hometown. Matthew and Josiah Brody. Trouble tends to follow them wherever they go."

The Brody brothers' father had started drinking and lost his job at the mill after their mother died giving birth to Josiah. Maybe that was the root of their troublesome ways. Still, it didn't give them the right to bully others and break the law. Pa always said to be kind and love everyone, but how could that apply to the Brody brothers?

Daniel tugged on Hannah's hand to leave, but she just swayed with the music and smiled. He blew out a breath and decided to stay. *Hannah shouldn't have to miss out on the fun because of those crazy loons.*

Daniel stared at Matthew chewing the stem of a dandelion as the fiddler's tune filled the night air. Matthew's gaze met his. The Brody boy shifted his focus to Virginia and Hannah. When the song ended, the lad twirled the dandelion stem between his fingers.

"Hey, Miss Virginia," Matthew called out. "I was sure surprised when your pa took on Mr. Keseberg today. Your pa can really whip his weight in wild cats."

"From what I hear," Virginia drawled out, "Mr. Keseberg deserved it."

"Nah." Mathew shook his head. "The big German's not such a bad egg."

Daniel chimed in. "Well, I certainly didn't care much for the way Keseberg talked about the Indians." He glanced at Hannah. As far as he knew, his stepsister's encounters with Indians had all been good. He hoped to protect her for as long as possible from hearing anything bad about them.

The seventeen-year-old Brody chewed his stem again. "Well, I happen to agree with Keseberg. The best Injun's a dead Injun. Haven't you heard about how, in his pioneering days, Daniel Boone had a son who was savagely murdered by them heathens? And, later, one of his daughters was kidnapped by another group of savages. I say we're better off without the whole dang lot of 'em."

Daniel stole another look at Hannah and saw her lower lip tremble. Recalling how Mr. Reed stood up to Keseberg, Daniel lifted his chin. "Just like there are bad whites and good whites, so there are bad Indians and good Indians. You can't just throw them all into one pot."

Matthew spat out his dandelion stem. "Well, as far as I know, there's no such thing as a good Injun."

"Then I guess you don't know very much," Daniel shot back.

An Irish lad named John Breen spoke up. "Play us another jig, why don't ya, Patrick?"

Daniel recognized John from the previous night when he and Morgan repaired a wheel on the Breen's wagon. While he appreciated John's attempt to calm the situation, he really wanted to take a swing at Matthew.

Matthew put a hand on the fiddler's arm. "Take a look, everybody." He pointed at Daniel. "We have an Injun lover among us." He sneered at Daniel. "Some folks say that's what got your daddy killed. Looks like you and him was cut from the same cloth. And what about your stepsister? Didn't she once live with the dirty savages? I wonder who *her* daddy was."

Daniel's emotions boiled over. He released Hannah's hand and, in one swift motion, dove toward Matthew, landing his fist in his stomach.

The Brody boy doubled over, gasping for breath.

Oh my God, what have I done? Daniel jerked back.

John Breen whispered to Daniel. "Matthew's always a pain in the arse, but I think you should leave now while ya still can."

"You're gonna regret that, Injun lover." Matthew moved toward Daniel and swung a fist at his face.

Daniel jumped out of reach, leaving his opponent batting the air. Daniel shoved him to the ground and turned to leave, but Matthew grabbed his leg, causing him to crash headlong into the dirt. Matthew flung himself on top of him and pinned his hands to the ground. Daniel thrashed his legs and managed to flip himself over. Matthew fell off to the side.

"You're done for, Whitcomb." The seventeen-year-old

growled as he crouched in front of Daniel. "Josiah! Give me a hand here!"

Daniel glanced up. Josiah approached with an upraised knife.

"That's enough!" A loud voice rang out.

Josiah stuffed his blade into his coat pocket.

The wagon master, Colonel Russell, pushed aside the crowd that had gathered to watch the fight.

"There'll be no fisticuffs on my wagon train," Colonel. Russell bellowed. "Get back to your families. Now!"

Grabbing Hannah's hand, Daniel headed back to their campfire with Jim and Eliza.

The next day, no one mentioned Daniel's fight with Matthew but, as Daniel had learned from Jim, from now on he'd be prepared for anything. Especially when it came to the Brody brothers.

S.T.E.A.M.

Watch the Britannica video at:
https://www.britannica.com/topic/Oregon-Trail

Answer the questions on Student Worksheet F1A Encyclopedia Britannica Video at:
https://drive.google.com/file/d/1o-QVZ2BMNR2m_sOcOLK75-LzlkxAQMlJk/view?usp=sharing

Continue with the Wagon Train Project at:
https://www.mariesontag.com/resources/teacher

4

THE WEDDING

June 16–23, 1846
Russell Wagon Train
Unorganized Territory

Daniel snapped his guide stick over the oxen. "Gee!" The oxen moved forward and to the right as he brought their wagon into line behind the others. A slow smile crept across his face. Morgan had promised to drive the wagon today so he could hunt with Jim.

The jangling of a harness and rattling of wagon wheels announced the arrival of another wagon. Daniel turned. Behind him, Morgan walked beside Miss Brisbin's wagon.

"Haw," Morgan shouted to the Brisbin's oxen. The animals swerved left. "Whoa!" he shouted again. The oxen pulled up behind Daniel's wagon.

"Miss Brisbin's father doesn't feel well," Morgan said as he approached Daniel. "So I offered to drive their wagon today. Figured you wouldn't mind putting off your hunting plans until tomorrow."

Daniel's eyes narrowed and his lips pinched. Of course

31

he minded. He tried to think of a snappy response, but nothing came to mind. He shrugged. Just one more broken promise to add to the list.

Miss Brisbin appeared from behind her wagon.

"See?" Morgan gestured toward Daniel. "I told you he'd be fine with it."

Miss Brisbin flashed Daniel a grateful smile. He didn't bother to return one.

Once again, Hannah walked beside Virginia as they plodded across the Great Plains. With no one to talk to, Daniel considered his future. *What happens to Hannah and me if Morgan gets serious about Miss Brisbin?* He had no answer.

When they stopped for their midday meal, Daniel and Hannah joined Morgan, Jim, and Jim's wife Eliza near the Savage's wagon. Eliza spread a white tablecloth on the ground. Everyone sat, except for Hannah. Standing, she tapped Morgan's shoulder and pointed in the direction of the Reed's wagon. She then pointed to her mouth.

"You want to eat lunch with the Reeds?" Morgan asked.

A smile flicked across her face as she nodded.

Daniel sighed. Eventually, the California trail would split off from the Oregon trail and they would part ways with Virginia and the families in the Donner-Reed group as they head for California. Morgan, Jim, and his cousins were determined to settle in the Oregon Country. Although it pleased him that Hannah had found a friend, it broke his heart to know she'd eventually add Virginia's name to the growing list of people to whom she'd have to say goodbye.

Morgan patted Hannah's head. "No, dear. I need you

to eat with us this afternoon. I have something to discuss with you and Daniel."

Daniel's mind raced. *What does Morgan want to talk about?* The way the man's gaze flitted from one person to another reminded him of something his father used to say. *He looks more nervous than a long-tailed cat in a room full of rocking chairs.*

Everyone except Morgan started in on the midday meal of dried jerky, cold biscuits, and wild berries. Morgan stood, cleared his throat, and placed his hands on his hips. "Daniel and Hannah, I have some great news. In two more days, Miss Frances Brisbin and I are to be married."

Daniel widened his eyes and willed his racing heart to slow. "Congratulations." He tried to smile, but his mouth refused.

Hannah pressed her soft hand into his.

"What will happen to us after you marry Miss Brisbin?" Daniel asked.

Morgan bit his upper lip. "Jim and Eliza have agreed to become your guardians. It seems Frances is not ready for an immediate family of two children. Jim and I signed an agreement this morning. Colonel Russell notarized it."

Daniel glanced at Jim.

The man simply nodded.

Daniel gazed at Eliza's protruding stomach. Like flies around a horse's tail, Daniel's thoughts shifted from one unanswered question to another.

Sure, we'll be part of Jim and Eliza's family until the baby comes. Then what? And what about my apprenticeship as a blacksmith? Without more blacksmith training, he doubted he'd be able to take care of Hannah once they reached the Oregon Country. And he'd never be able to save up enough money to go back to Illinois and find out who killed his parents.

"I have one more piece of news," Morgan added. "When we reach the Wyoming Territory where the Oregon Trail splits from the California Trail, Jim and Eliza have decided to stay with the wagons headed for California. I'll continue on with the Brisbins to the Oregon Country. Seems Jim fancies the life of a California storekeeper more than that of an Oregon farmer." Morgan's words tumbled out faster. "Before the wedding, I'll move my things to the Brisbin's wagon. You and Hannah can have the wagon and oxen you and I've been driving."

Daniel raised his eyebrows. Morgan's offer seemed generous. What little inheritance he and Hannah received from their father had paid for half of their wagon and supplies, and Morgan had paid the other half out of his own pocket. Now, Morgan was giving everything to him and Hannah.

Morgan scratched his clean-shaven jaw. "Over the next few weeks I'll show you as much as I can about blacksmithing till we reach Little Sandy Creek where the trail splits. Once you settle down in California, you might wanna consider working with Jim to develop trading posts instead of becoming a blacksmith. But it's your choice."

Daniel seemed to hear *it's your choice* a lot from the Savage brothers, and yet, since his parents' deaths, he barely had any say in what happened to him. He ate the rest of his midday meal in silence.

That evening, Eliza began to plan a special after-wedding supper. He always hated crowds. He didn't look forward to either the wedding or the special supper.

While Daniel gathered wood and buffalo chips for the evening fire, Eliza asked Jim to review their guest list. "Of course, there will be Morgan, Miss Brisbin, her brothers and widowed father, and Daniel and Hannah."

"Don't forget my cousins," Jim added.

"Of course." Eliza nodded. "We should also invite the Reeds. They've graciously offered to prepare pies for dessert. Then there's also Dr. and Mrs. Arnold."

Jim withdrew a corncob pipe from the inside pocket of his black overcoat. "Who are they?"

"Dr. Arnold's an eye doctor from England who was also once a minister. He's going to officiate the wedding."

Jim packed his pipe with tobacco. "We should also invite Mr. and Mrs. Boggs."

Eliza tucked a loose strand of hair behind her ear. "My, our list is getting long. Who are the Boggs?"

"Mr. Boggs was the former governor of Missouri. Heard rumors he might take over as wagon train master once we reach Fort Laramie." Jim paused to light his pipe. "Word is, Colonel Russell plans to step down as wagon master so he and a few others can travel the rest of the way to California by pack animal. They'll get there much faster."

Daniel's mind whirled as he lit the evening's fire. Sweaty palms, blurred vision, breath that caught in his throat—feelings surfaced that reminded him of the first time he swung across the wide creek behind his house. *Does Colonel Russell think the journey from Fort Laramie to California is too hard for the wagons? How many more plans will change before we get to where we're going? What if we never get there?*

Daniel stood to halt the wave of questions.

A few days later, by late afternoon, the wagon train reached the South Platte River crossing. Colonel Russel halted the travelers and advised them to form their usual circle. Those attending the Brisbin-Savage wedding gathered just outside the encampment. Dr. Arnold took his place in front of the crowd, while Morgan and his bride stood in front of him. Miss Brisbin, dressed in a blue cotton dress with a rounded ruffled neckline, clutched a handful of wildflowers Hannah and Virginia had gathered.

Everyone donned their least-ragged apparel. The men slicked back their hair and several women added a ribbon or two to their hair or outfits. Virginia looked especially fetching in her pink taffeta dress with its bell sleeves edged in white lace. Daniel wished he'd worked a little harder to get the stains out of his dingy white muslin shirt.

After the ceremony, Daniel found or borrowed various logs, benches, and buckets from fellow travelers so all the guests would have a place to sit. Soon, the guests gathered around the Savage's campfire for the evening meal. The fragrant aroma of cooked fish and venison made Daniel's mouth water. Eliza had also baked bread and Mrs. Reed gave them butter Virginia had churned from their cow's milk. After the meal, Eliza and Hannah served coffee and cream to go with the Reed's gooseberry pies.

As Daniel shoveled the last bit of pie into his mouth,

Dr. Arnold strolled over and sat on a log next to Hannah.

"I'm getting a little weary of just talking with the adults around here," he told Hannah. "Mind if I visit with you for a moment?"

Hannah shook her head no.

Daniel studied Dr. Arnold's thinning gray hair and bushy silver mustache. The man seemed nice enough and he enjoyed hearing the doctor's British accent.

Dressed in black woolen trousers, a white shirt, black vest, and an unbuttoned jacket, Dr. Arnold rested his hands on his knees. "Miss Hannah, I hear you don't feel like talking much these days, and that's just fine. I can do all the talking for both of us if you'd like. Lord knows, there have been times in my life when I didn't feel much like chatting. I find it rather nice to take a break from it once in a while. I suppose that's what you are doing."

Hannah nodded.

"You probably saw me at the wedding," Dr. Arnold continued. "When I was young, I once pastored a church in England, so today I was happy to perform the wedding ceremony. These days, I'm a doctor who treats people with special eye problems. My brother and father moved West several years ago, and my wife and I finally agreed to move out there with them."

Hannah tugged on a few loose strands of her honey-colored hair, smoothing out a section to make sure it covered her right eye.

"Oh, I don't mind seeing your eye that goes off to the side a bit," the doctor said. "In fact, if it is all right with you, I would like to ask about your eye. You see, I think I might be able to help you get it working again."

Even though the evening had cooled, a trickle of sweat worked its way down Daniel's back. Would Hannah think the doctor was getting too personal? He glanced at her. Her cotton-stuffed doll was tucked into the pocket of the white apron she wore over her blue and white calico dress. She pulled the one-armed doll from her pocket and clutched it to her chest.

"I dare say, that looks like a very special doll." Dr. Arnold pointed at the figure. "Does it have a name?"

Hannah crinkled her nose and nodded. She looked over at Daniel with wide eyes.

"She named her doll *Huhawira*," Daniel explained. "It means *moon* in the Ho-Chunk language."

"I see." Dr. Arnold pressed his spectacles closer to his face. "Do you mind if I take a closer look?"

Hannah held it up for him to see.

The doctor traced a finger over the threads that served as the doll's eyes, and the blank place where a mouth had worn off. "I see *Huhawira* doesn't feel like talking much right now either."

Frowning, Hannah shook her head.

"And it's missing one arm. Perhaps Mrs. Arnold could help with that. She loves fixing things and she is very good with a needle and thread. She worked as a seamstress in her younger days."

Hannah nodded.

"And now, Miss Hannah, would you mind if I took a closer look at your eyes?"

She swept back the lock of hair hiding her right eye.

"I dare say, you have beautiful blue eyes. Can you close your left eye for me?"

She closed it.

Dr. Arnold held up two fingers. "Can you tell me how many fingers I'm holding up?"

Hannah shook her head no.

"So, for now, your right eye is on holiday."

Opening her left eye, she nodded.

"Well, I don't think it's fair for your right eye to make your left eye do all the work, do you?"

Hannah looked down and shook her head.

"If it is all right with you and your brother, I can show you some things that might help your right eye do its share of the work. What do you think?"

She vigorously nodded yes.

Another bead of sweat trickled down Daniel's back. "Sir, I don't think you should give my sister false hope. And, besides, we can't pay for your services."

Dr. Arnold stood. "I wouldn't think of charging you, son. These types of problems are my specialty. And I believe I can help."

The doctor turned to Hannah. "I can't promise that your right eye will wake up, but there's a good possibility. With special treatment and exercises, you might regain some of your vision. Are you willing to try?"

She squeezed her eyebrows together and nodded.

Hannah and Daniel met with Dr. Arnold every day when the wagons stopped for the midday meal and every evening after chores. The doctor put Hannah through a series of eye exercises, sometimes with her right eye covered, sometimes with her left eye covered.

One evening after Hannah went to bed, Dr. and Mrs. Arnold sat with the Savages around their campfire and invited Daniel to join them. Everyone drank coffee, while the doctor and his wife sipped tea.

"Doctor," Daniel asked, "do you really think Hannah will be able to see again out of her right eye?"

The older gentleman cupped his hands around his ceramic teacup. "Son, I don't think Hannah has true vision loss. I believe she suffers from what is called a *lazy eye*. The right eye, for whatever reason, stopped teaming with the left, and, from what you've told me, it probably began around the time she and her mother went to live with the Ho-Chunk Indians."

Daniel swatted a mosquito feasting on the back of his neck. "Why would living with the Ho-Chunk affect her eyes?"

The doctor placed his teacup on the tree stump next to him. "You see, Daniel, God made our brains very complex. If our brain receives confusing information, parts of the brain can shut down in order to cope. Because Hannah's right eye began to move independently from her left, it gave her confusing visual information. Eventually, this caused the right eye to stop working in order to avoid this confusion. If we can strengthen the muscles in her right eye and help it move closer to the center, her right eye's vision might return."

Daniel's pulse picked up its pace. For the first time since leaving Illinois, he felt hopeful. "That would be wonderful, Dr. Arnold. And what about Hannah's speech? Does that have anything to do with her eye problem?"

The doctor retrieved his teacup and sipped. "It's possible. Right now, her brain is like an overly distracted horse that has trouble responding to its master's commands. With the loss of her father, living with the Indians in a new culture and having to learn a new language, and then her right eye not teaming with the left, I believe her brain found it hard to cope. Getting her right eye to track with the left would be a first step in clearing up her brain's confusion."

"Is there anything else I can do to help?" Daniel asked.

Dr. Arnold stroked his bushy mustache. "Are there any routines your family had at home you could continue out here on the trail?"

Daniel frowned. "Ma and Pa used to read to us every night from the Bible, but our Bible got burned up in the fire along with everything else."

Mrs. Arnold clucked her tongue. "I picked up an extra Bible when the Bible Society was handing them out to pioneers before we left Missouri. You're welcome to it."

He'd seen the Bible Society in Missouri pass out free Bibles to the wagon train pioneers, but he hadn't taken one. He knew his parents believed they were doing God's will when they stood up for the Indians or helped escaped slaves, but, since his parents' deaths, he didn't want to listen or talk to God anymore.

Encouraged by Dr. Arnold's insights, Daniel promised to read the Bible every night to Hannah and to help her each day with her eye exercises.

On some days, the doctor instructed Hannah to wear a patch over her left eye from noon until they stopped for the evening. On those days, if Daniel was busy guiding their wagon's oxen, Virginia acted as Hannah's guide. She would hold Hannah's hand as they walked alongside the wagon train.

One morning when Hannah had both eyes unpatched,

Jim asked his cousin, Charles, to guide Daniel and Hannah's oxen so he and Daniel could hunt. When Hannah got wind of it, she motioned that she wanted Daniel to spend the day walking with her and Virginia. Although he really wanted to hunt, he reluctantly agreed to accompany the girls.

After several minutes of walking in silence, Virginia struck up a conversation. "So, Daniel, Mrs. Savage tells me you like to read. Do you have some favorites? Are you reading anything right now?"

Daniel plodded on in silence. He really didn't want to talk. His feet hurt and the hot sun baked out what little energy he had left. He'd much rather be hunting than listening to Virginia's chatter. A mosquito pricked his arm. He slapped it away. Finally he broke the silence. "Yeah, I like reading."

More silence.

"Well, I'm reading *Robinson Crusoe*," Virginia volunteered. "Have you read it? Some people think it was a true story written by Robinson Crusoe, but it's not. Even though it's not real, it's fun to read."

"Uh huh."

More silence.

Virginia pressed on. "Did you know that Mrs. Boggs is a granddaughter of Daniel Boone?" She stopped to pick a flower. "Mrs. Boggs loaned me a book about Daniel Boone written by Timothy Flint but I haven't had time to read it yet."

Virginia had finally caught his attention. "Really? Mrs. Boggs is related to Daniel Boone? I had that Timothy Flint book, but it got burned up in the fire."

"I'm sure Mrs. Boggs wouldn't mind if I loaned it to you."

"I'd like that very much." He wiped sweat from his

forehead with the back of his hand, then slapped away another mosquito.

Virginia and Hannah stopped to pick flowers, but he continued to trudge forward.

That girl sure does talk a lot.

A few minutes later, Virginia and Hannah ran to catch up with him.

Lengthening their steps to match his pace, Virginia and Hannah showed Daniel their handfuls of primroses and larkspur.

"I think friends are like flowers," Virginia said. "They add sunshine and color to your life. Don't you agree?"

Daniel shrugged. "Sometimes, I think friends are like mosquitos. They buzz around in your ear, waiting to take a bite out of you, then leave behind an itch you really shouldn't scratch."

Virginia frowned. "Well, that's a pretty sad view of life. Before this trip is over, maybe you'll come to see friends as more of a flower than a mosquito."

"I'm just telling you what I think." He shrugged again. "You don't have to agree with me."

Virginia grabbed his shirtsleeve. "Let's stop for a minute. I have something to show you."

Daniel blew out an exasperated sigh, but paused as Virginia withdrew a book from her apron pocket.

"This is my father's book," Virginia said as she held it up for him to see. "It's called, *The Emigrants' Guide to Oregon and California.*" She opened to where she'd inserted a dried dandelion and pointed to a drawing. "According to this, we should be able to see Chimney Rock soon. It's one of the landmarks along the trail."

Daniel hooked his thumbs under his suspenders and leaned over to examine the drawing. He still thought Virginia was more like a mosquito than a flower, but he admired her adventurous spirit. He scanned the left and right sides of the trail.

"I don't see any unusual rock formations around here." He tried to sound authoritative, but only managed to squeak out the words.

Why does my voice have to crack right now? Isn't there anything I can control?

The morning hours ticked by with sporadic conversation. By the time Daniel's stomach growled announcing lunchtime, he spotted the clay and sandstone pillar of Chimney Rock off to the left. It stood atop what he estimated to be a 300-foot mound.

Virginia ran ahead, leaving Daniel to trail behind with Hannah. When he and Hannah reached the rock, Virginia was carving something into the chimney's sandstone column.

"What are you doing?" He leaned in for a closer look.

"I'm cutting our family's name into the rock. See the names of all the other pioneers who've passed by here?" Virginia pointed with the tip of her hunting knife to several names inscribed in the stone.

As she continued to carve, Hannah shook Daniel's arm and pointed at the names.

Daniel drew his brows together. "You want us to put our names here too?"

Hannah nodded. "Names."

Hannah had spoken! Daniel wanted to jump up and down, but figured it might embarrass his stepsister. He glanced at Virginia. Her wide eyes told him she'd also heard.

"Oh, my." Virginia enveloped Hannah in a hug. "It's so good to hear your precious voice!"

Daniel took out his pocketknife and scratched into the stone, *Daniel & Hannah Whitcomb*.

S.T.E.A.M.

Continue with the Wagon Project at:
https://www.mariesontag.com/resources/teacher/

5

FORT LARAMIE

June 23–27, 1846
Fort Laramie
Unorganized Territory

"Moving sand. That's what some emigrants call the Platte River," Jim explained one morning as he and Daniel rode ahead of the wagons to hunt elk.

Daniel loved these rare moments when Morgan drove their wagon and he got to ride alongside Jim on his spare horse.

"The Platte River's slow," Jim continued, "but it gives us a route to follow through the Unorganized Territory. Unfortunately, we'll have to cross and re-cross it several times before we get to Fort Laramie."

Having ridden for about two hours, Jim slowed his horse to a walking gait. Daniel adjusted to meet his pace.

Jim glanced over at him. "Remember when we crossed that wide creek back in the Kaw Indian territory? Now *that* was an adventure."

Daniel nodded. That crossing remained permanently

etched in his mind. He had ridden with Jim, Mr. Reed, and Mr. Breen in search of a place where the wagons could cross a creek on the Great Plains, but everywhere they looked, sharp cliffs barred any descent to the creek bed. In the end, they had to lower the wagons and oxen down the steep banks with ropes in order to reach a crossing point where they could continue their journey west. Using hooks and lines, they got the wagons down, but had to double up teams of oxen to haul the wagons and their contents up the opposite bank.

"Think there'll be more Indians out here like the Kaw we met in the Kansa Indian territory?" Daniel asked as they followed a bend in the river.

"I doubt it," Jim said. "Them Kaw Indians out there on the Great Plains were in a sad state. I warned Colonel Russell not to camp so close to their village, but he wouldn't listen."

Jim picked up the pace, and Daniel goaded his horse to keep up.

When Jim slowed once more, Daniel continued to reflect. "The Kaw sure looked a lot different than the Ho-Chunk back home. I have to admit, seeing pieces of bone, tin, and brass hanging from their ears or noses scared me at first." He recalled waking up that morning to find the Kaw roaming through their camp as they begged for clothes, food, buttons, or whatever struck their fancy.

"I felt sorry for them," Daniel added. "So many were dressed in just dirty blankets and leggings. Virginia said her ma gave them and an old pair of Mr. Reed's pants, along with some bread and jerky. Seeing most had tangled and matted hair, Virginia asked if she could give them one of her hairbrushes, but her ma said no. She wasn't sure they'd know how to use it."

"I think we all felt sorry for them," Jim said.

"Why don't those Kaw hunt for their food like most other Indians?"

"They used to," Jim said. "But, with trappers and emigrants traipsing through their territory, the game's been driven farther and farther west. Before long, the Kaw'll have nothing to eat but roots and berries."

Daniel shook his head, trying to dislodge the scene from his mind.

A few days after Jim and Daniel hunted elk, the wagon train came to a point in the Platte River where rocks and cliffs blocked their way, forcing them to cross the river. Since the water was high, some men swam the cattle over while others built rafts. The women unpacked the wagons' goods to make it easier to raft the wagons across. Once the rafts were sent back, the pioneers shipped over the wagons' contents. The men re-greased their wagon wheels on the other side, and, after repacking their goods and re-harnessing the oxen, they returned to the trail.

Exhausted from the day, many went to bed early once they made camp. Daniel had promised Dr. Arnold he'd read to Hannah every night from the Bible. After supper, however, all he wanted to do was crawl under the blankets in their wagon bed and fall asleep.

As they prepared to turn in, Hannah brought him the Bible and tugged his sleeve. "Read, please."

Daniel widened his eyes. Hannah hadn't said another word since that day at Chimney Rock. How could he refuse?

The next day as the pioneers neared Fort Laramie, Daniel saw hundreds of war-painted Indians gathered near the trading post waving hunting knives, tomahawks, bows, and arrows. He urged his oxen forward until they pulled alongside Jim's team. Over the din of rattling chains, lowing oxen, and men's voices, he figured Jim wouldn't hear him ask about the scene in front of them, but at least he'd be closer to his guardian in case of trouble.

Daniel knew Fort Laramie wasn't a military post. At least that's what Jim told him. Built with wooden logs, it had served as a trading post for the early wilderness men who trapped beaver. Now, it was a place where those traveling west could rest and stock up on goods.

Daniel's shoulder muscles tightened. Would the Indians attack the wagon train before it reached the fort? Were the natives preparing to storm the post? After seeing the sad state of the Kaw, he could hardly blame them if they did.

Hannah tromped next to Daniel through the beaten down grass as he flicked his guide stick across the backs of their oxen. Would the sight of these war-painted Indians cause Hannah a set-back? Daniel glanced at his step-sister as she surveyed the mass of Indians spread out on the plain. She grabbed the sleeve of his flaxen shirt and pulled him close.

Daniel shouted at Jim. "What's going on?"

As if straining to hear, Jim placed a hand behind his ear.

Daniel shouted again.

Handing his guide stick to his cousin, Jim strode over to Daniel. "Those are Sioux Indians," Jim shouted as he got closer. He pointed toward the braves near the fort. "They're about to do a war dance, I reckon. Probably plan to fight the Crows or the Blackfeet. Nothin' to worry about."

Nothing to worry about? Indians fighting each other didn't sound like "nothing to worry about." Daniel flicked his guide stick again, its snap lost in the surrounding ruckus.

Off to the right, a party of mounted warriors, two abreast, trotted past the wagons. The Indians carried green twigs between their teeth and solemnly tossed them to the pioneers as they rode by.

Daniel glanced at Jim with raised brows.

His guardian laughed. "Don't worry. It's a sign of friendship. They mean no harm."

Walking behind the warriors came a procession of beautiful Indian girls dressed in white doeskins. They had bright colored beads sewn onto their neatly trimmed dresses.

By mid-afternoon the wagon train, too large to camp within the fort's walls, formed a circle as close to the fort as possible. Daniel hoped they'd rest at the trading post for a few days so they could repair wagons, resupply their food stores, and launder clothes.

Colonel Russell and a few other men had already left by pack mule to head for California. Mr. Boggs, the new wagon master, said they'd only spend one day at the fort. "We need to keep moving so we can stay on schedule."

That evening, after reading to Hannah and tucking her into bed, Daniel groused to Jim around the campfire. "Staying at the fort for only one day won't give us enough time to purchase provisions and make our necessary wagon repairs."

Jim pulled out his corncob pipe and stuffed it with tobacco. "We'll have to attend to our animals and wagons further up the trail." Jim lit his pipe and began to puff.

Eliza, having washed the evening's utensils, sat on the log next to Jim. "Hopefully, we'll also find a place to wash our dusty, trail-worn clothes."

The next morning, Mr. Boggs asked Jim and Mr. Reed to ride ahead in search of the best place to camp once they left Fort Laramie. Jim invited Daniel to join them. That gave him even less time to buy supplies at the trading post, but he agreed, leaving Hannah with the Reeds.

"Looks like the best place to rest is farther up the trail near Beaver Creek," Jim reported to Boggs once they returned.

"There's a natural bridge there where we can cross," Mr. Reed added. "We can reach Beaver Creek by July 4 and take time to celebrate the holiday, while we give the oxen and cattle a chance to rest. The animals can graze while we repair our wagons and wash clothes."

From discussions he'd heard around the campfires, Daniel knew both the animals and the humans needed a few days to recoup before tackling the upcoming trails through the South Pass of the Rocky Mountains. Eliza especially needed rest. He had hoped her baby would come by the time they reached Fort Laramie. It hadn't.

After an early supper, Daniel checked his oxen, then sat with Hannah near the fire. With a woolen blanket draped over their shoulders, he opened the Arnold's Bible to where he'd left off the previous night, the gospel of St. John.

Let not your heart be troubled: ye believe in God,
believe also in me. In my Father's house are many

mansions: if it were not so, I would have told you. I go to prepare a place for you. And if I go and prepare a place for you, I will come again, and receive you unto myself; that where I am, there ye may be also.

As the sun sank lower in the sky, Hannah ran her finger over the words, *a place for you.* She snuggled closer to him. "Sounds wonderful," she whispered.

"Soon we'll have a place to call home." He ruffled her hair. He hoped she believed him. He wasn't sure he believed himself.

Jim tapped his shoulder. "Mr. Boggs has invited a few of us, including you, to meet with a Mr. Clyman inside the fort tonight. Seems Clyman has a message for us about the shortcut Mr. Reed's been talkin' about from that book of his."

Daniel inhaled, drinking in a sense of pride.

After reading to Hannah, Daniel went to the post to purchase supplies. Inside the storeroom he saw goods such as flour, dried beef, beans, coffee, jams, blankets, and tools. The post's proprietors also sold weapons such as knives, guns and rifles. After setting aside flour, salt, and beans, he picked up one of the .50-caliber Hawken Plains rifles.

"Think you'd like to buy one of those someday?" Jim asked.

"Yes, sir. I sure would."

Jim didn't know it, but he'd already set aside a store of cash. He hadn't planned to buy a rifle with it, however. Since only a few blacksmiths accompanied the wagon train, he and Morgan's services were always in demand. The travelers paid them well, and Morgan let him keep a good share of the money. He wondered if Morgan felt guilty for shirking his guardianship duty, but Daniel really didn't care. He wanted to save as much as possible so one day he could return to Illinois.

Putting down the rifle, he fingered the deer-bone handle of a Bowie knife. It's curved, keen point, heavy, broad blade, and S-guard that could catch an opponent's blade while protecting the user's hand made it a valuable weapon in combat. He thought of the way Hannah grasped his arm yesterday as she watched the war-painted Sioux parade near the fort. Yes. He could afford to buy the knife.

"Them's the best for clearing a path, butchering game, or fightin' Injuns."

Daniel turned and found himself staring into a bearded, weathered-looking man who towered at least a foot above him.

Dressed in buckskins, the large man patted a sheathed blade at his side. "I reckon my Bowie's saved my life more times than I can count."

"Yes, sir," was all Daniel could manage to say.

The man walked to the counter and pulled two gold coins from the leather pouch at his side. "A bottle of your best whiskey," he told the proprietor. "And give me a few whiskey glasses to go with it."

Daniel picked up the Bowie knife and added it to his other purchases.

"Gentleman." The weathered-looking man said, surveying the other pioneers inside the post. "Glad you came. Got important information to pass along." He pointed to a round table near the back of the room and. "Let's sit over there." He brought over his bottle of whiskey and several short glasses that clinked together. The group followed.

Chairs scraped across the rough wooden floor as the men sat.

"Name's James Clyman." The man removed his beaver fur hat and settled into a chair next to Daniel. Pouring whiskey into the glasses, he placed one in front of each man. He paused when he set a glass in front of Mr. Reed.

"Well I'll be," Clyman said. "And how are you, ya' old possum? Ain't seen you since the Black Hawk War of '32." The man paused to sip his whiskey. "Those Sauk Injuns back east sure do look a might different than the Injuns out here, don't they?"

Clyman didn't wait for a response. Still studying Mr. Reed, he asked, "And how's our old friend, Lincoln? When d'ya see him last?"

"Abe?" Reed pushed aside his glass of whiskey. "A lot's happened since the Black Hawk Wars. Abe married in '42, and before we left Springfield he was hoping to win an Illinois seat as a U.S. Representative. I haven't heard yet if he won, but I wouldn't be surprised. You know how he was when we fought together during the Black Hawk Wars. When that man sets his mind to something, he sees it through."

Clyman nodded and glanced at the other men around the table. "The reason I asked y'all to meet me is 'cause of this half-baked plan of Hastings. I hear tell some of you have it in your heads to take Hastings' supposed shortcut after you reach Fort Bridger next month." The mountain man withdrew a crinkled, hand-drawn map from the pocket of his buckskin shirt. He smoothed it out and traced a finger along the line labeled Hastings Cutoff.

Shifting in his chair, Mr. Reed fingered his whiskey glass without taking a sip.

Daniel cocked his head. He'd seen this shortcut in Mr. Reed's book written by Mr. Hastings. Virginia had shown him Hastings Cutoff and said her father planned to take it because it would shorten their trip by about 350 miles. On paper, it made sense.

Mr. Reed cleared his throat. "As a businessman, I believe it would be smarter to take the Hastings Cutoff. The sooner we reach California, the sooner we can set up homes and businesses."

"Ya know me, James." Clyman scratched his scraggly brown beard. "I've always said, money ain't everything. It won't do ya no good to take the shortcut in order to make more money if ya ain't around to spend it. I've heard tell that Hastings hisself ain't even traveled this cutoff."

Running his hand through his silver hair, Mr. Boggs spoke up. "I have heard it rumored that Hastings wrote his book just to encourage Americans to move to this unsettled Mexican-owned area in hopes of starting a bloodless revolution. People say Hastings has it in his head to make himself emperor of this area once American settlers seize the land from the Mexican government."

Mr. Reed arched a brow. "The way Texas became its own country ten years ago?"

Clyman nodded.

Leaning back in his chair, Mr. Boggs hooked his thumbs in his vest pockets. "Mr. Clyman, as a seasoned mountain man, what do you think? Is Hastings just promoting this cutoff to get more people to move West?"

Once again, Clyman nodded. "He's sendin' people on a fool's errand. Hastings' so-called shortcut takes you 'cross the Great Salt Lake desert where there's no water for about

150 miles. And some of them canyons is so steep, you'll have to pull your wagons up the cliffs with ropes and chains. Mark my words. Hastings' shortcut ain't no shortcut."

Daniel's stomach summersaulted at the thought of having no water for 150 miles.

"But Clyman," Mr. Reed said. "We're already about a week behind schedule. We've got to get through the Sierras before the snows come. If not, we'll get trapped there for months."

"It's your choice, men." Clyman shook his head. "If the shortcut is all Hastings says it is, it'll surely save you almost 400 miles of travel. You'll make it to California at least a month sooner than them that go the regular route. But if Hastings' cutoff is what I think it is, you might never reach California."

Later that evening, Daniel found it hard to sleep. When he did drift off, he dreamed of marauding Indians, dry deserts, and impassable mountains. Would he and Hannah be safe with whatever decision Jim and the others made? Maybe their former leader, Colonel Russell, had chosen the best course—abandon the wagon train and travel by donkey to California with just a small group of trusted people. Daniel hoped the morning would bring a sense of clarity.

S.T.E.A.M.

Complete the Student Map Worksheet, F1B Map at:
https://drive.google.com/file/d/1kAr6Ab-pyRbcnboD-gh1IblYOoQJkDO8I/view?usp=sharing

Continue the Wagon Project at:
https://www.mariesontag.com/resources/teacher/

6

BEAVER CREEK

June 28–July 5, 1846
Fort Laramie to Beaver Creek

The next morning, the wagon train continued to follow the trail west.

Five days later, Virginia sat with Hannah and Daniel around the Savage's evening campfire, about twelve miles east of Beaver Creek. She read to them from Hasting's guidebook.

"Here's where he talks about Independence Rock." Virginia leaned closer to the firelight. "Even though we won't reach Independence Rock in time to celebrate the 4th of July, the guidebook tells how the large rock got its name. It says, 'If pioneers reach this large, granite mound by July 4th, they have a better chance of making it through the Sierra Nevada Mountains before the autumn snowfall prevents further travel.'"

Jim puffed on his pipe, then exhaled a sweet-smelling smoke. "Well, we're still about eleven days from Independence Rock. Since we won't reach it by July 4, Mr. Boggs says we'll celebrate the holiday at Beaver Creek. We'll camp there for two days to rest up and prepare for the next leg of the journey."

On the morning of July 4, the pioneers reached Beaver Creek at about 11 a.m. While Eliza and Hannah prepared lunch for their little family of four, Daniel and Jim unyoked the oxen.

Virginia ran up, huffing, as if out of breath. "You're all invited to join us at our wagon for lemonade at noon. Pa has a surprise he's sharing with the men to toast Independence Day, and Mama will treat the rest of us to lemonade."

Eliza patted Virginia's shoulder. "Tell your Ma and Pa we'd be delighted to join them. The 4th of July is always a special day for our young country."

By noon, a crowd gathered near the Reed's wagon. Mr. Reed held up a green, glass bottle ornamented with a ridged relief of grapes and vines. "Upon our departure, my Springfield friends gave me this bottle of brandy. They suggested I offer a toast at noon on the 4th of July to celebrate the holiday. They said they'd offer a similar toast for us back home at the same time."

Daniel fully intended to drink lemonade at the celebration, but when Mr. Reed offered him a small glass of brandy, and Jim nodded his approval, Daniel stood a bit taller. He slowly sipped his small portion. He held back a look of disgust as a sweet, burning taste slipped down his throat and into his stomach.

Mrs. Reed and Mrs. Donner led the group in singing various patriotic songs, including *Hail Columbia, My Country 'Tis of Thee*, and *The Star Spangled Banner*. Although

Hannah didn't sing, Daniel's heart leapt to see a faint smile touch her lips.

Eliza and Hannah brought food to join the Reeds in their noonday meal. Virginia told Daniel and Hannah about all the things she hoped to do when they reached California.

"I'm gonna ride horses, go to dances, buy fine dresses, and marry a rich man."

Daniel shook his head. *Girls.*

When the hot July sun beat down on them, they moved to the shade of a nearby tree. By the time they finished lunch, sweat had soaked the back and armpits of Daniel's long-sleeved muslin shirt. He excused himself and ambled over to the creek for a swim. On the way, he heard shouting behind the Keseberg's wagon. Curious, he crept closer, careful to remain hidden behind a wagon wheel.

Mr. Keseberg grasped a bottle of whiskey in one hand and his wife's arm in the other. "*Ack.* Do not lecture me, woman!" Mr. Keseberg shook his wife's forearm and pushed her away.

Mrs. Keseberg took a step back, lost her footing, and fell to the ground.

Her husband waved a dismissive hand. "I deserve to have a good, long drink. Leave me alone."

The two Keseberg children cowered on the ground next to Mrs. Keseberg, their eyes wide as they clung to her apron. They began to whimper.

Mr. Keseberg took another drink from his half-empty bottle. "And get the *kleinen Kinder* to shush. I cannot abide their bawling!"

His wife stood, lifted the baby boy into her arms and

grabbed her daughter's pudgy little hand. "Perhaps if you talked to the children in a gentler voice…"

The large German strode over and slapped her face. "Do not speak to me in that tone, woman." He lifted his hand as if to strike again.

Daniel ran between them. "Mr. Keseberg." More sweat dripped down his back. "Ah, I want to ask you something." He glanced up into the large man's red-rimmed eyes. His mind raced to think of what to say next. "Ah, I want to ask, do you plan to take the Hastings Cutoff along with the Reeds and the Donners?"

Behind him, Daniel heard the crackling of dried twigs. He inhaled a shaky breath, hoping Mrs. Keseberg and the children had slipped out of harm's way.

Grabbing the front of Daniel's shirt, Mr. Keseberg yanked him closer to his face. The man's foul breath made him gag.

"Mind your own business, boy, or I will to give you a taste of what I gave my wife."

John Breen came around the side of the Keseberg wagon.

Daniel exhaled a sigh of relief.

"Ah, there you are Whitcomb. I've been a-lookin' all over for ya. Mr. Savage says you was a-headin' to the creek."

Before Daniel could reply, John stood at his side. "We'll be takin' leave of you now, sir." The Irish lad tipped his cap at the German and pulled Daniel toward the creek.

"That was none too smart," John said once they were out of earshot. "What were you a-thinkin', taking on a man twice yer size? T'was even more stupid than takin' on Matthew Brody. Do you have a death wish, my friend?"

"I couldn't just stand there and watch that bully beat

his wife." Daniel wiped sweat from his forehead with his shirtsleeve. "How can she live with a man like that?"

John shook his head. "Maybe she's used to it, or perhaps 'tis just their way. To be sure, I don't know. But that was a right good way to get yourself killed, interferin' like that."

"But it's not fair!"

"Life's not fair, Danny boy. You've got to play the hand you're dealt."

"Well, it stinks."

John laughed as they reached the creek. "You're right about one thing. Somethin' 'round here surely stinks." John playfully sniffed the air near Daniel. "Ahh, 'tis you!" John shoved him into the cold creek.

Daniel lost his footing and went under. A second later he popped up and, like a wet dog, shook his full head of brown hair.

John stood on the muddy bank and laughed.

"Oh, you've gone and done it now, Breen." Daniel scrambled up the embankment and grabbed John's leg. A second later, both boys thrashed in the water as they splashed and dunked each other.

Daniel felt a small stone hit his shoulder, then another hit his head. "Hey!" he yelled as he glanced around. There on the bank stood Matthew Brody, a dandelion stem pinched between his teeth. Josiah stood next to him, holding a bottle of whiskey.

Matthew threw another pebble at Daniel, but it fell short. "Look!" Matthew said to Josiah. "There's a couple of little beavers in the creek. Let's see if we can scare 'em out so we can skin 'em alive."

A larger rock flew into the creek and splashed between

Daniel and John. Daniel slapped a swipe of water at Matthew. "Why don't you come here and see if you can catch me with your bare hands?" He sneered. "Or maybe you're too scared."

Matthew grabbed the whiskey bottle from Josiah. "Not till we finish this. Thanks to findin' my daddy's hidden stash, we're celebratin' the 4th of July in style."

Daniel swam toward the embankment. "Well, then, maybe I'll just come up there."

John reached out and grabbed Daniel's shirt, pulling him back to the middle of the creek. "I've no doubt you could take on both them boys," John said close to Daniel's ear. "But I've no stomach for a fight, 'specially since they've both been a-drinkin'. Let's just, as you Americans say, *skee-daddle*."

Daniel and John sloshed through the water to the far side. Matthew and Josiah laughed as they continued throwing stones.

That night Mr. Boggs placed six people on guard duty around the camp. In addition to Daniel, he assigned John Breen, Mr. Reed, Mr. Donner, Matthew, and Mr. Brody. Although the travelers had yet to experience any trouble from Indians, Boggs warned the guards to keep a sharp lookout. Earlier that day, scouts saw a small band of Cheyenne roaming the area. Jim loaned Daniel his Hawken rifle, and John Breen brought along his father's flintlock pistol and field dressing knife.

Daniel held Jim's rifle across his chest as he strode to his assigned spot. A few hours later, he gazed up and saw two shooting stars sweep across the sky. *God, what an amazing world*. A wolf howled in the distance. As he focused on the sound, he heard the faint squeak of bats navigating through the night.

A twig snapped.

He froze.

He glanced at his surroundings, now faintly bathed in moonlight. He saw nothing. *My mind's playing tricks on me.*

A cool breeze touched his cheek.

Another crack.

He tightened his grip on the rifle.

Everything went black. Someone flung a burlap bag over his head, stripped him of his rifle, and yanked his arms behind his back. Struggling to free himself, a punch to his back brought him to his knees.

"Mmm. Scalp 'em. Steal cattle," a low voice said.

"Mmm." Another said.

Daniel's breath caught in his throat. He assumed his attackers were Cheyenne. With his arms still forced behind his back, one of his opponents yanked the bag from his head and grabbed a handful of his hair. The cold blade of a knife pressed against his hairline.

Oh, my God! They're going to scalp me!

Daniel thrashed his legs and managed to roll to his side. He wished he'd also brought his Bowie knife.

His attacker fell on top of him and pressed a knife blade to Daniel's throat.

Lifting back his head, Daniel bit his opponent's hand. He sensed the iron-like taste of blood as he sunk his teeth into his enemy's flesh.

The stranger howled and dropped his knife. The other attacker scurried to retrieve it.

Now free, Daniel scrambled to his feet, but a punch to his stomach brought him to his knees. Several blows to his kidneys and a kick to his head dropped him to the ground. Once again, the world went dark.

"Danny boy, wake up."

From somewhere far away came a familiar voice, but he couldn't place it.

"You okay, my friend?"

He opened his eyes. It was still dark out. His whole body throbbed with pain. Slowly rising to a sitting position, he touched a tender area on the side of his head. *At least I still have hair on my head.* Next to him stood John Breen. Daniel moaned as he looked up at his friend. "What happened?"

"You tell me," John said. "The sun will be up soon. Our watch is almost over. I called out for ya, but I didn't hear ya answer. That's when I saw you a-lyin' here."

Daniel groaned again and tried to stand. "I think I was attacked by Indians. Did they steal any cattle?"

John reached out a hand and helped him up. "Can't tell in this light. You sure t'was Injuns?"

Daniel stood and blinked a few times. "Yeah. They said something 'bout scalpin' me. Guess they changed their minds or got scared off."

Daniel searched the area for Jim's Hawken and spied it a few feet away. "At least they didn't take Jim's rifle." As he walked over to pick it up, Daniel's foot kicked something else in the grass. He leaned down and picked up an empty bottle. In the dim light of the rising sun he read the label. Old Overholt.

Daniel and Morgan spent the morning heating and refitting wagon wheels. After a month of driving, many of the wagons' iron rims had grown loose as their wooden wheels shrunk with the heat. They reheated the iron bands to tighten them. As he worked, Daniel stewed about the identity of last night's attackers. Having found the Old Overholt bottle, he suspected Matthew and Josiah Brody, but he couldn't prove it. For now, he'd just focus on the work at hand.

In the afternoon, Matthew and Josiah's father enlisted Daniel's and Morgan's services. "Two of our oxen threw shoes," Mr. Brody said. "Of course, I'll pay ya for the work."

Daniel didn't want to help the Brodys, but he could use all the money he could earn. Besides saving for the future, he hoped to buy some cloth for Hannah when they reached the next trading post. In addition to the trip's wear and tear on their clothes, Daniel also noticed Hannah had experienced a growth spurt in the past month. Some of her dress seams had ripped open. He asked Mrs. Arnold if she'd make dresses for Hannah if he bought the material, and she gladly agreed.

As Daniel and Morgan stoked a hot fire to make shoes for Brody's oxen, Morgan told Matthew and Josiah to dig a trench.

Matthew whined. "Ahh, what for? Since we're payin' ya, isn't that yer job?"

Morgan pounded the piece of metal in his vice. "Shoein' an ox ain't the same as shoein' a horse. To shoe an ox, we gotta turn him upside-down in a trench so we can get to his hooves. It ain't possible to raise an ox's leg the way you do a horse. While we're gettin' things ready, we need you to dig a deep furrow."

Daniel forced himself not to snicker as he listened to Matthew and Josiah grumble about digging a trench. He also caught Mr. Brody smile as the man stood on a stool to sew a torn area on his wagon's canvas. Their pa also seemed to enjoy the spectacle.

Once the boys finished the trench, Mr. Brody helped Daniel and Morgan tie ropes around one of the oxen's legs. Working together, they flipped the animal into the shallow pit. With the ox on his back, Morgan and Daniel filed its shoeless hoof and reshod it. They did the same with the second ox.

When finished, Daniel passed by Matthew and bumped his shoulder. "Seems there's more to takin' down an ox than a person." Daniel kept his voice low. "Can't just throw a bag over it and knock it on the head. Not without some kickback. Truth be told, I got a bit of ox in me."

Matthew stared at Daniel with raised eyebrows. Either Matthew was surprised that he'd guessed he was one of his attackers, or Matthew was trying to pretend he didn't know what Daniel was talking about. Either way, he'd let Matthew know he suspected his part in last night's beating, and that he could expect payback. He relished the flicker of fear that briefly flashed across Matthew's face.

S.T.E.A.M.

Finish the Wagon Project at:
https://www.mariesontag.com/resources/teacher/

7

HASTINGS CUTOFF

July 5–20, 1846
Beaver Creek to Fort Bridger

That evening, just before supper, three mountain men dressed in fringed buckskin coats strolled into the pioneers' camp. All three had long, scraggly beards. Two pack mules trailed the trio. Daniel joined the Boggs, Savages, Donners, and Reeds who gathered around the newcomers.

"Welcome to our camp." Mr. Boggs extended a hand to the man with the longest beard. "What brings you our way?"

Outfitted in a coonskin cap, the man returned Boggs' handshake. "On our way back to the states to sell these here pelts." The trapper jabbed a crooked thumb toward the donkeys loaded with beaver skins and supplies.

"I'm Lillian Boggs, leader of this wagon train," Mr. Boggs introduced himself.

"Name's Dodger," the trapper said.

The second man, whose wide-brimmed hat looked as though it had been stomped by an ox and dragged through the mud, stepped forward. "They call me Hawk." He also shook Boggs' hand.

"And this here"—Dodger pointed to a man whose face look less weathered than the other two—"this here's Meek."

"We're about to prepare supper." Eliza stirred a pot hung over their campfire. "If you'd like to join us, we've got plenty to share."

"Why, that's right neighborly, ma'am." Dodger's wide smile revealed a chipped front tooth. "We'd be mighty grateful."

Hawk removed his felt hat and dusted it off on his thigh. "If any of you've got letters you'd like to send to the states, we'd be happy to drop 'em off at the nearest post office."

Mrs. Donner put a hand to her mouth, then lowered it. "That would be wonderful." She scurried to her wagon while Mrs. Reed, Mrs. Boggs, and Eliza discussed what they'd each contribute to the evening meal. Daniel brought over more buffalo chips for the fire.

A moment later, Mrs. Donner returned with several sheets of paper. "I'd be much obliged if you'd mail these to the *Springfield Journal*." She stuffed the pages into a make-shift envelope. "The editor said he'd print any account of our journey I managed to send his way." She scrawled the address on the front and handed it to Hawk, along with a gold coin.

Hawk handed the coin back. "There's no cost, ma'am. Consider it our thanks for servin' us a home-cooked meal, so to speak."

"Oh!" Virginia's eyes went wide. "Mama, can I send Cousin Mary a letter?"

Mrs. Reed smiled. "Of course, dear. I'm sure Mary would be delighted to hear from you."

Virginia turned to the trappers. "You *are* planning to

spend the night in our camp, and leave in the morning, aren't you? That'll give me time to write my letter."

Dodger nodded. "Sure, miss."

Just before supper, Daniel wrote a letter the trappers could mail to Pastor Lovejoy.

Dear Pastor Lovejoy,

You'll be glad to hear that Hannah is starting to speak. And Dr. Arnold, an eye doctor travelling with our wagon train, is trying to help her eye problem. Maybe both things will eventually get fixed.

I wish I could get fixed. I feel like my insides are twisted up something fierce. I'm mad that we couldn't find out who killed my parents before we left. I'm mad that a large German in our wagon train beats his wife. I'm mad that one of the young men traveling with us picks on me and says bad things about Indians and my parents. You might remember him. Matthew Brody. He, his brother, and their pa are travelling with our wagon train to California.

I want God to judge these people. I want life to be fair, but it's not. You once told me not to look for justice on my own. You said it would eat me up. I'm afraid that's what's happening. I don't know what to do. I don't know how much longer I can hold on without taking matters into my own hands. Even though you can't write to give me advice, it feels good to get things off my mind.

I forgot to tell you. Morgan got hitched. His new bride wanted Morgan, but not us. Morgan's going with her to the Oregon Country when the trail splits.

He got his brother Jim to be our guardian. I'm glad. Jim's taught me how to shoot, skin animals, and many other things I never learned. Jim changed his mind about going to Oregon. When we get to The Parting of the Ways, we'll go with him and all the other people headed to California.

I hope this letter finds you and your family in good health.

Your friend,
Daniel Whitcomb

After supper, the women went back to their wagons. Hannah sat next to Daniel as they listened to the men swap stories with the trappers around the Savage's campfire. The pioneers talked about their journey, and the trappers shared stories about grizzly bears, Indians, and starving for weeks while trapped in the Sierra snows.

During a lull in the conversation, Daniel turned to Dodger. "Know anything 'bout the Hastings Cutoff?"

Dodger scratched his bushy gray beard. "I knew pioneers who took it," he said. "Everyone I talked to 'bout it urged against it."

"I was hoping we'd go that route," Mr. Reed said. "We're behind schedule, so I figured we'd get to California by way of Hastings Cutoff. As you've mentioned, we need to make it through the Sierras before the deep snows hit."

Hawk withdrew a pipe from his coat pocket and packed it with tobacco. "I've heard tell that James Bridger's been promotin' Hastings' shortcut. Truth be told, Bridger tells travelers to take that cutoff 'cause it's good for his tradin' post business."

"How's that?" Mr. Boggs leaned in.

Dodger pulled a map out of his coat pocket. Unfolding it, he nudged Jim to hold one side while he held the other.

With dusk stealing more of the evening light, Daniel moved closer to get a better look.

"Here's where we're at now." Dodger pointed to an area just east of Independence Rock. "Used to be, emigrants headin' to Oregon or California stayed together far as Fort Bridger. Then they'd head north to Fort Hall. Now, with the discovery of the Greenwood Cutoff, there ain't no need to go as far south as Fort Bridger."

Mr. Reed moved over to study Dodger's map. "But what if we drive our wagons south to Fort Bridger, then brave the Hastings Cutoff?" Mr. Reed drew his finger over the route from Fort Bridger to the shortcut, and then west to where it joined up with the California Trail. "Wouldn't that shave about 350 to 400 miles off our trip?"

Dodger scratched his beard. "Nah. More like you'd save 250 to 300 miles. Either way, less miles don't necessarily mean less trouble, or less time."

Mr. Reed frowned.

"Besides," Dodger added, "I hear Hastings ain't even traveled that way hisself. Rumors be, he's in cahoots with Bridger. Hastings tells people to take his shortcut so Bridger can make more money from those who come to his trading post before taking the cutoff. But those who've taken his so-called shortcut say it's filled with steep cliffs and thick groves of trees. If ya make it past all that, ya still gotta cross 150 miles of barren desert. On the other hand, if ya take the Greenwood Cutoff, there's only 'bout 50 miles of waterless desert."

Jim shook his head. "Sounds like Hastings' shortcut's a bad decision."

Daniel draped Hannah's blanket more securely around her shoulders. "Especially if Hastings and Bridger are only promoting it to make money."

Mr. Boggs glanced over at Virginia's stepfather. "Mr. Reed, don't you recall our discussion with Mr. Clyman at Fort Laramie? He also warned us about taking Hastings' route. It seems the wiser course to take the Greenwood Cutoff and drive the wagons to Fort Hall instead of Fort Bridger."

The more Daniel listened to the trappers, the more the Hastings Cutoff sounded like the wrong decision. Daniel knew the Breens and Donners would probably do whatever Mr. Reed did. For Hannah's sake, he hoped Jim would join Mr. Boggs in traveling the extra miles to Fort Hall.

By July 11, Daniel, along with Jim's family and cousins, passed Devil's Gate. Daniel and Jim were riding back to the wagon train after bringing down a buffalo when Daniel saw the granite formation in the distance.

"Why do we have to go around these mountains to get to the other side?" Daniel readjusted his grip on his horse's reins as they trotted closer to the wagons. "Why can't we just go through Devil's Gate?"

Jim glanced west, shading his eyes against the glare of the afternoon sun. "You can't see it from here, but the Sweetwater River flows through that gap they call Devil's Gate. Pioneers who've traveled this way say the opening's only about thirty-feet wide. The canyon's barely wide enough for the river to pass through, much less the wagons. Gotta go around the mountains to get to the other side."

As they drew closer, Daniel counted the wagons. Twenty. They included the Donner-Reed group, the Arnolds, Brodys, Jim's cousins and relatives, and Daniel and Hannah. The other forty or so wagons with Mr. Boggs were now about two days ahead of them.

Daniel wanted the wagon train to stay together in case of an Indian attack. As Jim said, there was safety in numbers. But, after leaving Beaver Creek, Eliza developed a fever and Jim slackened his pace. Mr. Brody and Dr. Arnold were also sick. Those in the Donner-Reed party traveled more slowly because, like the Reeds with their double-decker wagon, they pulled heavier loads than the others in Boggs' group. Their situation reminded Daniel of the tortoise and the hare. In his case, however, he wished he was the hare.

The trail between Devil's Gate and the South Pass gradually ascended, slowing the group's progress even more. By the time their lagging group crossed the summit of the Rocky Mountains, they received word from advance scouts that those traveling to California with the Boggs, as well as the parties headed to the Oregon Country, had already taken the Greenwood Cutoff and were on their way to Fort Hall. When Daniel heard the news, he realized he hadn't said goodbye to Morgan. Had Jim?

Four days later, they reached the Greenwood Cutoff. After an early supper, Daniel sat with Hannah, Jim, Dr. Arnold, and Mr. Reed by the Savage's crackling campfire. The women had already returned to their wagons.

"So, gentleman. What route shall we take tomorrow?" the doctor asked. "Should we take the Greenwood Cutoff, following the Boggs' train north to Fort Hall, or should we go south to Fort Bridger and then take the Hastings Cutoff over to the California Trail?"

"You already know my thoughts." Mr. Reed's voice came low but firm as he poked the fire with a stick.

Jim packed his pipe, lit it, and puffed several times. "Whatever we decide, we should all agree. Let's suggest that all the men and boys over fourteen vote on it tonight. We should all agree with the majority vote."

Dr. Arnold nodded. "That sounds like a wise plan. How will you vote, Jim?"

His guardian glanced at Mr. Reed. "With Eliza still sick and the baby due any day, I vote we follow the Boggs wagons. We should take the Greenwood Cutoff, go north to Fort Hall, then west to California."

"Ah." Dr. Arnold gazed into the star-lit sky. "To quote a line from Shakespeare, *I fear some consequence yet hanging in the stars shall bitterly begin our fearful date.* I suspect that may happen no matter what route we take."

Daniel drew his brows together and pondered Dr. Arnold's words. He didn't understand what they meant, but he didn't ask him to explain. Like a coon up a tree, he felt trapped. Since he was still only thirteen, he couldn't vote. If he could, he'd certainly vote to avoid the Hastings Cutoff. He abandoned the men and strode with Hannah to their wagon.

As Daniel tucked her in, she pointed to the Bible on top of a sack of flour. "Psalms tonight."

Daniel smiled. She spoke more every day. He turned up

the wick in the oil lamp, picked up the Bible, and opened to Psalms 16. It was one of his stepmother's favorites.

> *I will bless the Lord who has given me counsel;*
> *My heart also instructs me in the night seasons. I*
> *have set the Lord always before me; Because He is*
> *at my right hand I shall not be moved.… You will*
> *show me the path of life; In Your presence is fullness*
> *of joy; at Your right hand are pleasures forevermore.*

Hannah's face beamed. He hadn't seen her angelic face light up that way in a long time.

"What'cha smiling 'bout, Sassafras?"

"Not scared anymore."

He shot her a puzzled look.

She patted an area to the right of her pillow and pointed at the Bible. "God." Once more she tapped the area next to her pillow. "Right here."

Daniel read the passage again. "Because He is at my right hand I shall not be moved." He nodded. "You mean you're not scared anymore because you feel God is right beside you?"

Hannah nodded, pulled in a fast breath, and yawned. "Sleepy now." She tugged her gray woolen blanket up around her chin and turned to face the shadowed canvas wall. "Night, Daniel."

He reached over and handed Hannah her doll, its arm and mouth now repaired, then leaned in to kiss her cheek. "Night, Sassafras."

"Night, Daniel." She hugged his neck, then kissed her doll. "Night, *Huhawira.*"

Daniel stepped out of the wagon and shook his head, amazed at Hannah's childlike faith. He wished he was as sure of God's presence as she was.

Fullness of joy in God's presence? I haven't felt that in a long time. Guess that means I'm not in God's presence. At least, not like Hannah.

He gazed up at the stars. The evening sky reminded him of the dark, pin-pricked cloths they'd hung over the windows two winters ago when his family had the flu. The semi-darkened room helped them rest more easily during the daylight hours. Tonight's stars gave him only minimal guidance as he made his way to his bedroll beneath the wagon. *God, at least show Jim the path of life as he takes us to California. Help him choose the best route for Eliza and us. And please watch over Jim. I'd be lost if anything happened to him.*

The next morning as they broke camp, Daniel quizzed Jim about last night's vote.

His guardian's lips pulled into a frown. "Most voted to go south to Fort Bridger."

Daniel readjusted his oxen's harness. "Then I guess Mr. Reed got his way. At least Hannah and Virginia won't have to say goodbye. She can travel the rest of the way to California alongside her friend."

For the next few weeks, the words of Mr. Clyman back at Fort Laramie haunted him. *Mark my words, men. Hastings' shortcut ain't no shortcut.*

The closer they drew to Fort Bridger, the more the Donner-Reed group fell behind. By the time Daniel, the Savages, the Brodys and the Arnolds reached the post, those in the Donner-Reed group trailed them by about five days.

Jim and the others waited at the post a few days, hoping the others would catch up, but by July 20, the small group at Fort Bridger was ready to move on. A wagon train of forty wagons led by a man named Harlan had also rested at the trading post. They too were eager to leave. Mr. Harlan invited Jim's group to join them. They all agreed.

Daniel picked up another bag of flour as he and Jim purchased the last of their supplies inside the trading post. "Can't we wait a few more days?" Daniel placed the bag next to the counter and handed Mr. Bridger a gold coin. "The Reeds should be here shortly." He glanced at Jim. "It would mean a lot to Hannah."

"Sorry, Daniel." Jim paid for his ammunition. "It's better we move out early tomorrow morning. Seems Mr. Hastings himself promised to lead us through his shortcut. Can't afford to wait another few days. I'm sure Hannah can meet up with Virginia once we get to California."

The next morning while harnessing their oxen, the Donner-Reed party arrived. "See." Daniel pointed to the wagons. "I told you they'd get here in time."

Jim frowned. "Like us, they'll need to stay at the fort a few days to rest up and resupply. But we need to leave now."

While Daniel re-checked his harnesses, John Breen came over.

"Sorry we couldn't get here sooner," John said. "You be sure now to watch out for them Brody boys."

Daniel shook John's hand. "I will, 'specially since you won't be around to keep me safe."

The Irish lad laughed. "Ah, we won't be far behind ya.

Maybe we'll catch up with each other at Sutter's Fort."

After John left, Virginia and Hannah said goodbye. The girls hugged, cried, then hugged again.

"I'll miss you somethin' fierce," Virginia told Hannah. "If we don't meet up with each other at Sutter's Fort, Pa says we'll head to Mission San José. I'll try to leave word for you there or at Mission Santa Clara as to our whereabouts. Pa hasn't decided yet where we'll finally settle."

Hannah hugged Virginia again. "Thanks, friend." She wiped her tears with the back of her hand.

"Thanks for being my friend too, Hannah. Even though you didn't talk much, I guess I talked enough for both of us."

Virginia had seemed bossy and strong-headed, but Daniel had come to respect and admire her honesty and adventurous spirit. He'd miss her too.

Just then Virginia glanced up. Her eyes met his.

His knees went slack. Chewing his lower lip, he strode over. Grabbing Virginia's hand, he shook it. "Miss Virginia, I was pleased to make your acquaintance." *Too formal.*

Still pumping her hand, he tried again. "I mean, I'm glad our paths crossed."

He really wanted to tell her how pretty she looked and that he hoped they'd see each other again soon. Instead, he continued to shake her hand.

Virginia giggled. She grasped Daniel's arm and stilled his handshake. "Yes, I'll miss you too." She cocked her head to the side. "And, have you decided?"

Daniel narrowed his eyes. "Decided what?"

"If I'm a mosquito or a flower."

His cheeks flamed with embarrassment. He gazed at the ground.

"A flower," he muttered.

She leaned forward and kissed his cheek. "So are you." She smiled. "I'm sure our paths will cross again. Soon, I hope."

Tightness gripped his stomach and moved to his throat. He let her hand drop and lightly punched her shoulder. "Well, until then. Um, uh…" he floundered to find the right words, but none came to mind. "Well, have a good life."

Have a good life? Daniel berated himself, unable to think of something to say that didn't sound stupid. He wanted to say goodbye, but couldn't push out the words. He'd said goodbye too much this past year. Ma and Pa, Pastor Lovejoy, Morgan. Turning back to his wagon, he grabbed his guide stick. "Come on, Hannah." His voice came out thick. "Time to go."

Hannah and Virginia hugged once more.

Virginia turned and walked back to her family's wagon.

With Hannah at his side, Daniel guided his oxen to follow along behind Jim and Eliza's wagon. He wished he'd also given Virginia a hug.

S.T.E.A.M.

Begin the S.T.E.A.M. Project at:
  https://www.mariesontag.com/resources/teacher/
for Chapters 7-8, Arts Connection

8

THE WASTACH MOUNTAINS

July 20–early August 1846
Fort Bridger to Devil's Gate

"So much for the Hastings Cutoff." Daniel groaned as he and Jim used their Bowie knives to slash back the shrubs and saplings that blocked their path through the Wasatch Mountains. "I bet we're making only one, or at the most, two miles a day." Although he complained about their slow progress, Daniel almost welcomed the sting of his calloused hands and overworked muscles. In a strange way, his physical pain seemed to lessen the phantom pain between his ribs—the pain of missing Virginia.

Jim nodded. "Guess those mountain men were right after all. This shortcut ain't no shortcut at all."

The next day, Matthew and Josiah's pa confronted Hastings. "You lied to us about this shortcut, Hastings. We're goin' so slow, we'll probably get trapped by snow when we reach the Sierras."

Hastings' nostrils flared. "You're welcome to leave the wagon train any time you'd like, sir."

Brody slammed his fist into Hasting's jaw.

Hastings reeled back. He wiped blood from his lip. Clenching his fists, the wiry man put equal weight on each foot as he took up a fighting stance.

Was the man too stupid, or too proud to realize he didn't stand a chance against Brody? Matthew and Josiah's pa probably outweighed Hastings by at least 75 pounds.

Brody raised his chin, inviting Hastings to take the first swing.

The wagon master jumped between the two. "Gentlemen, we're all hot and tired. Fighting ain't gonna help. We gotta keep moving."

The next day, after Daniel awoke, Harlan called a meeting. "Mr. Hastings rode off early this morning. Said he had another wagon train at Fort Bridger he needed to lead through the cutoff."

"Sure." Brody sneered. "More like he feared for his life if stayed with us."

A few days later, the Arnolds joined the Savages for their midday meal. Daniel nibbled on his hardtack biscuit, then used it to push his beans around his tin plate. He sucked in a few breaths, but felt like he couldn't get the air to fully reach his lungs.

"Are you not feeling well, son?" Dr. Arnold asked. "I've never known you lose your appetite."

"I don't like the feel of this so-called trail, Dr. Arnold." His chest muscles tightened. "What if we get trapped in the Sierras by a snowstorm, like Mr. Brody said? I'm having trouble breathing, and I can barely sleep at night."

"I have confidence Mr. Harlan will get us through."

Dr. Arnold scooped up the last of his beans. "As for your breathing, you're just not used to the altitude, son."

Daniel quirked a brow.

Dr. Arnold wiped his silver mustache with his handkerchief. "As we get higher into the mountains, the air thins out. Eventually, our bodies will adjust. I wouldn't be too concerned."

By July 27, they finally reached Weber River. Daniel found it easier to breathe. Although the river lay in a deep canyon, at least they could follow it to the Great Salt Lake.

After four days of travel, the river narrowed. "Watch your footing on those bushy banks," Jim shouted to Daniel as they guided their oxen and wagons beside the swift-flowing river.

In spite of Jim's warning, Daniel twisted his ankle as they trudged over the rocky, uneven ground. Twice, he slipped into the foamy, roaring waters.

A few days later, they made camp on the south side of the Weber where it opened up to a flat plain. On the north side of the river, a wall of granite loomed above them. Eerie shadows, cast by their campfires, danced across the cold stone, just as foreboding thoughts of fear danced across his emotions.

The next morning, according to the daily rotation plan, Daniel pulled his wagon up behind Mr. Harlan's rig. Dr. Arnold and Jim followed behind Daniel. After about three miles of travel through the river's upper gorge, large boulders appeared, blocking further passage. Daniel moaned. How would they be able to move forward now? Every muscle in his body ached.

Harlan halted the wagon train and addressed the group. "Men! Form teams of five. We'll lead the animals through the river and lift the wagons over each boulder."

Several groans arose, but everyone followed Harlan's instructions.

After an hour of sloshing through the icy waters and clambering over rough boulders, Daniel couldn't even wiggle his toes. They felt frozen inside his water-slogged shoes. As he raised his guide stick to direct the oxen, fiery pain shot through his right arm from overuse. He choked back the bile that rose to his throat and turned his head from Hannah in case he lost his midday meal. If they didn't stop soon, he feared his pain and fatigue would make him vomit.

Later that evening, after warming his feet by the fire and drying out his thin-soled shoes, Daniel stopped by the Arnold's wagon. "Got anything to soothe my aching feet?" He pulled back his sock to reveal two angry red blisters, tender to the touch. "Sure do wish we'd gone with Mr. Boggs' group to Fort Hall."

Dr. Arnold retrieved his black medicine bag from the back of his wagon. "Things are bound to get better soon." He withdrew a jar of salve and handed it to Daniel.

Sitting on a rock, Daniel unscrewed the lid. "I doubt it." He winced as he dabbed his wounds with the ointment. He shuddered at the overshadowing fear that things would get worse before they'd get better.

Two days later, they rounded a bend in the river. Daniel brightened at the view ahead. The canyon's watercourse widened, made a sharp S-curve, then straightened out for quite a distance. "Look, Hannah," he pointed toward the scene. "Maybe things will get easier now. Why, my blisters might even have a chance to heal!"

As he predicted, for the next seven days, the banks of the widened river offered an easier trail.

At midday the following week, Harlan halted the wagons. In front of them stood a vertical rock wall about seventy-five feet high, rising up from the middle of the riverbed. Closed in by the canyon, how would they ever get beyond the rock wall?

"So much for an easier path," he complained to Hannah.

Harlan walked down the line of wagons. "Buck up, boys! We've conquered all obstacles so far. We'll conquer this one too."

The wall looked higher than any tree Daniel had ever seen. He guessed it was higher than twelve to thirteen men standing on each other's shoulders. Harlan instructed the women and children to remove all the items from their wagons they could carry through the narrow passage between the river and the wall—the wall they had now named Devil's Gate.

"The horses'll squeeze through there too." Harlan pointed to the narrow passage. "But there's no way the oxen will. We'll have to haul them, along with the wagons, over the rock wall."

Daniel helped Hannah tie up some food supplies in a blanket and join the others as they pressed through the opening.

Harlan appointed the strongest men to climb to the top of the wall and secure ropes between trees so they could winch up the oxen and wagons. But he didn't ask Jim to go.

Daniel shot Harlan a puzzled look. Although Jim was

short, he was one of the strongest men in the group. Why didn't the wagon master assigned Jim to help winch up the wagons?

Harlan must have noticed Daniel's bewilderment. "I'm gonna need you and Jim at the bottom as part of the relief team." Harlan removed his kerchief from around his neck and wiped sweat from his forehead.

Confused, Daniel cocked his head.

The wagon master shouted out more instructions. "Reed, Brody, Smith, Benson, Ira, and John, space yourselves up the left side of the wall. Sift, Wright, Wimmer, Pyle, and Fowler, climb up to the right. When the men at the top crank up the wagons and oxen, be ready to help lift and guide the wagons up the wall."

As directed, Daniel stood next to Jim and several of the other men at the bottom. When some of the men on the rockface tired, Harlan replaced them with those waiting below. Finally, only five wagons remained at the bottom. Harlan replaced two of the men on the wall with Daniel and Jim.

Daniel clambered up to a spot with good footing about halfway up. Salty sweat stung his eyes as he strained to help lift the right rear wheel of a wagon over a deep crevice. When one of the last wagons and its team neared his position, a shout came from above.

"One of the ropes has worn out near the windlass! Hold on while we throw down two more ropes to loop around the wagon."

Several of the men from below scrambled up near Jim and Daniel, helping them lift the wheels and sides of the wagon in order to take pressure off the frayed rope. Daniel's grip on the wagon began to slip. Some of the men across from him struggled to find a new foothold. A few released their hold on the wagon.

"It's no use, men," Harlan shouted from below. "You'll have to abandon the wagon and the oxen, or be dragged to your death."

Daniel looked across his position at Jim. Surely they could hold on long enough to get the new ropes fastened around the wagon.

Jim shook his head.

Several men went slack-jaw.

Daniel swallowed hard.

Harlan shouted once more. "On the count of three. One, two three!"

The oxen, seeming to sense the danger, let out a baneful bawl. Daniel stepped clear as the men released their hold. Wood exploded as jagged wagon pieces clattered off the rocks like trees felled in an ice storm. The earth spasmed and sent vibrations up through the mass of granite where Daniel struggled to keep his balance on the narrow ledge. He gasped at the broken bodies of the fallen beasts whose muscles briefly quivered in the after-throes of death.

He didn't know the family who lost their wagon and animals in the crash, but he climbed down and helped them retrieve whatever they could—a frying pan, chisel, hammer, shovel, two pails, and chains from the animals' harness. He also helped Jim and several others butcher the oxen for the devastated family.

If the trail proved so difficult for them, how would Virginia's group ever be able to make it through?

S.T.E.A.M.

Continue the S.T.E.A.M. Project at:
https://www.mariesontag.com/resources/teacher/
for Chapters 7-8, Arts Connection

Also see Teacher Notes F1C_Teacher_Notes_
Chp_9_10.pdf

9

INDIAN ATTACK

August 10–late September 1846
Fort Bridger to Steamboat Springs

A few days out from Devil's Gate, the canyon opened up into a lush green valley. "We'll spend a few days here to rest," Harlan announced. "Let's use the time to cut and bundle grass, and fill all available containers with water. We'll need these for our next ordeal—the Great Salt Lake Desert."

"The desert." Daniel whined under his breath as he cut down swaths of grass and Hannah bound them with strips of braided buffalo sinew. "How in the world will we survive that?"

Hannah raised her eyebrows at him. "Remember, Virginia told us that Hasting's guidebook said we would get through the dessert in two days. That doesn't sound so bad."

He hadn't intended for her to hear him. He marveled at Hannah's positive attitude. He wanted to remind her that Hastings book had been wrong about everything else so far, but what good would that do?

By the third day of plodding through the desert, Daniel's tongue swelled. How much longer would their water hold out? He'd already grumbled to Jim, to Harlan, and to the Arnolds about Hastings' miscalculations, but criticizing Hastings didn't shorten the distance. There was nothing to do but to move forward.

"How ya doin', Sassafras?"

She gave him a faint smile. "Can't be much farther."

Her hardy spirit amazed him. For the past three days, Hannah had gone out of her way to make sure Eliza had everything she needed. She began to speak more, and her right eye moved closer to the center. When a snake slithered by, and then a scorpion crossed her path, she didn't shriek.

After two more days of nothing but desert, Daniel's chest constricted when he saw their water barrel was almost dry. Clouds of alkaline dust made it hard to see more than ten feet ahead. A fine powder had settled on their skin, causing it to burn. He found it almost impossible to put one foot in front of the other.

Finally, after six sun-blistering days, they arrived at a spring near Pilot Peak.

"Remember, drink slowly," Daniel reminded Hannah. "Dr. Arnold says if we drink too much or too fast, it could make us sick."

For the next two days, they rested at the spring. Jim and Eliza spoke very little. Aside from getting a drink or stretching her legs, Eliza spent most of her time resting in her wagon.

That afternoon, while helping Jim feed and water his horses, Daniel asked his guardian, "How's Eliza doing?"

Jim shook his head. "I 'spect the journey through the salt flats has taken a toll on all of us."

After caring for the horses, Daniel shuffled off to find Hannah. He found her at the Arnold's wagon, sewing clothes.

"Look, Daniel." Hannah held up the half-finished calico dress on her lap. "Mrs. Arnold let me make most of this one by myself." She handed the dress to Mrs. Arnold and retrieved a red-colored broadcloth from the back of the wagon. "And she showed me how to use berries to color the material you bought me at Ft. Bridger."

It brightened his heart that Hannah continued in good spirits, even though she didn't have Virginia. In addition to learning how to sew with Mrs. Arnold, she volunteered to do most of the cooking and washing in order to give Eliza time to rest.

After a few days at Pilot Peak, they moved on and reached the Humboldt River by mid-September. At the river, the summer weather quickly gave way to a chilly autumn. Harlan sent out two scouts to find rest spots for the next few nights. They returned to say they found the Boggs party about seventy miles ahead.

While Daniel stoked the evening fire, he overheard Jim tell Eliza, "If we'd taken the trail to Fort Hall with the Boggs party, we'd be almost six days closer to Fort Sutter. I'm so sorry, Eliza."

She merely patted her large belly as she and Hannah finished making the evening meal.

After two days of following the Humboldt River, Harlan assessed the group's remaining supplies and then called everyone together. "What with several oxen dropping in the desert and our unexpected delays, we can't possibly make it to California before running outta supplies."

Several women moaned. The men murmured among themselves.

"What are we gonna do?" one man shouted.

"I've asked my nephew, Jacob, and another young man, Tom Smith, to ride to Sutter's Fort for help." Harlan took a swig of water from his canteen. "They'll bring back cattle and provisions that'll get us through the rest of the trip. We'll meet up with 'em on the east side of the Sierra Nevada mountains as we begin our ascent."

Jacob and Tom took off by pack mule for Sutter's Fort while the group continued its slow trek toward California. Four days after Jacob and Tom left, Harlan halted the wagon train about an hour after the mid-day meal.

It was too early to set up camp for the night. Why were they stopping now? Daniel's muscles tensed. Whatever it was, it couldn't be good.

Hannah must have sensed the danger too. She grabbed Daniel's arm and stared at him with wide eyes.

"Hannah, why don't you check on Eliza."

She nodded, and ran up the line toward the Savage's wagon, her long blonde braid bouncing across her back.

Daniel, like Hannah, feared for Eliza's life, and that of her unborn child. A week ago he helped bury a woman who, Dr. Arnold said, died of mountain fever. Since then, Eliza, just like the other woman, developed a fever. And, yesterday, just like the other woman, flat pink spots appeared on Eliza's wrists and forearms.

Daniel stood next to his wagon and inhaled, hoping to fill his lungs with the fresh mountain air. He still found it difficult to draw in a deep breath. His limbs trembled as he walked to the side of the wagon and ladled himself a drink from the water barrel. As he sipped, Dr. Arnold ran up.

Daniel ladled a drink for the doctor. "Why have we stopped?"

Breathing hard, Dr. Arnold paused to swallow a gulp before he spoke. "Someone up ahead found a wooden board with a long message from the Boggs' party."

"What'd it say?" The water splashed as Daniel dropped the ladle back into the barrel.

"The message warned of Indian attacks." The doctor wiped his mouth with his handkerchief. "It seems a man in the Boggs party was killed, and another was badly wounded. Five days ago, a party of Paiutes attacked them with poisoned arrows. They think the Indians soaked their tips in rattlesnake venom. Three others who were shot began throwing up, had a rapid pulse, and displayed signs of numbness. Although caught off guard, the pioneers were able to fight back. Before the wagon train moved on, they estimate they killed about forty Paiutes."

Mr. Brody, having pulled up behind Daniel's wagon, joined the trio. "Why've we stopped?" he demanded. "It's not even dusk yet." The large man waved his arms. His face reddened. "We could still go another five or six miles."

"There's danger ahead." Dr. Arnold quirked his eyebrows. "Indians."

A few children in the nearby wagons began to cry. Their mothers tried to shush them. Sensing danger, the oxen began to bawl. As ordered, the pioneers circled their wagons and secured the animals.

Once everyone had settled, Harlan climbed atop a

boulder and addressed his fellow-travelers. "We've been warned of an Indian attack." Harlan's gaze scanned the huddled mass. "The Boggs' group is now about seventy-five miles ahead of us. They left a message saying the Indians in these parts mean to steal our cattle. Not that we've got much left to take. I know we're worn out from passing through the mountains and crossing the desert, and we're low on food and supplies. Hopefully, though, we'll receive help when Jacob and Tom return from Fort Sutter. Until then, keep a sharp lookout for trouble. Ration your food. And keep up your spirits."

"And pray," a woman in the crowd added.

"Amen to that," a man shouted.

After supper Jim wanted to stay with Eliza, so he asked Daniel to check on his horses and oxen.

"Of course." Daniel nodded. He turned toward Hannah before he left. "I'd like you to get ready for bed, Sassafras. When I get back, I'll read to you." Without waiting for her response, he grabbed his hat and took off for the area inside the circle of wagons where the horses had been hobbled.

Finding Jim's two mounts, he gave the first a biscuit.

"Can I feed them too?" a small voice peeped out from behind Jim's palomino.

Daniel looked around the golden-colored horse and saw Hannah petting its white mane.

He frowned. "What'cha you doin' out here, Sassafras? You should be gettin' ready for bed."

She pinched her lower lip between her teeth. "I wanted to see the horses, too."

Daniel handed her his other biscuit.

When Hannah finished feeding the palomino, she

rubbed her hands together and brushed off the crumbs. "I also wanna pick some wildflowers for Eliza. Wanna cheer her up."

Daniel shook his head. "Not tonight. You go get ready for bed. I'll be back after I check the oxen."

When Hannah opened her mouth to argue, Daniel raised a finger. She lowered her head and turned to leave.

Since there wasn't enough room inside the circle for the oxen to graze, the animals rested just outside the camp. Daniel was glad Harlan had doubled the number of guards they usually posted. Knowing Matthew and Josiah were among those on first watch, he decided to survey the camp's security before he checked the oxen.

Once outside the circle of wagons, Daniel scanned the area. He spotted Matthew and Josiah leaning against a tall pine about a hundred yards out. *Why are they just standing around? They should be spaced out, keeping watch for an attack.* Before he could whistle to get their attention, he saw Hannah out of the corner of his eye. *Why is she still here?*

As he headed in her direction, she began to pick wildflowers.

Suddenly, Matthew and Josiah raced towards camp. "Injuns!" they shouted.

Just as Daniel glanced over at them, an arrow sliced through Josiah's arm. The lanky youth stumbled. Matthew threw Josiah's good arm over his own shoulder to keep Josiah on his feet as they stumbled toward camp. A group of five bare-chested Paiutes, dressed only in breechcloths, chased after them. The Indians fired arrows as they narrowed the gap between themselves and the Brody brothers.

Daniel sped toward Hannah.

The Indians pursuing Matthew and Josiah changed direction and headed for the horses. All except one who bore down on Hannah's position.

"Get back to camp!" Daniel yelled at Hannah.

He tackled the young brave before he reached his sister.

The two wrestled on the grass. With sweaty hands, Daniel strained to maintain his grip around the Indian's bare chest. He managed to punch and knee the brave several times before the Paiute squirmed out of reach and yanked a knife from his belt.

Like a bear, Daniel charged, grabbed the Indian's legs, and toppled him to the ground.

The brave's knife flew out of his hand.

With one arm wrapped around the Indian's legs, Daniel whipped out his Bowie knife.

Hannah screamed.

Daniel shoved his knife into the Indian's chest.

The Paiute went limp and dropped to the ground.

Fearing his heart might beat right out of his chest, Daniel wrenched his knife from the Indian's torso. Both the knife and his hand were covered in blood. He slid the blade back into its sheath and turned to grab Hannah. She lay about ten feet away, the shaft of an arrow protruding from her chest.

"No!" he screamed.

Scooping her up, he bolted toward camp.

About fifty yards away, Indians fled with many of the horses and oxen in tow. He hid with Hannah behind a tree until they passed. The stolen horses and oxen didn't matter now. All that mattered was Hannah.

A doctor from the Harlan train treated Josiah's arm,

while Dr. Arnold rushed Hannah into his wagon to tend to her. An hour later, when darkness had settled over the camp, Dr. Arnold approached Daniel by the campfire.

He braced himself for the news.

"I'm so sorry, son." The gray-haired physician removed his spectacles. "The arrow…" His voice cracked and faltered. "The arrow damaged some of her vital organs. I couldn't…" His voice dropped as he turned to wipe his eyes on his shirtsleeve. "I couldn't save her."

Daniel's feet froze. His head buzzed. His limbs quivered like the day he lost hold of the wagon that crashed down the granite wall of the Weber River. In spite of how much he wanted to save that wagon, it slipped through his grasp. Staring into the fire, he refused to meet the doctor's gaze. Now Hannah had also slipped through his grasp.

Jim laid a hand on his shoulder. Daniel shrugged it off.

Dr. Arnold stepped closer. "It's a terrible thing, Daniel. I'm so sorry." The doctor's voice sounded gravelly and tired. "If there's anything Mrs. Arnold and I can do…" Dr. Arnold sobbed, cutting his sentence short.

Daniel tried to swallow the large lump in his throat, but it wouldn't budge. The emptiness in his chest threatened to consume him. "No doctor. There's nothing anyone can do now."

S.T.E.A.M.

Continue the S.T.E.A.M. Project at:
https://www.mariesontag.com/resources/teacher/
for Chapters 7-8, Arts Connection

Also see Teacher Notes F1C_Teacher_Notes_Chp9_10.pdf

If students are ready, begin Final Project. See F2_Final_Project_Handout.pdf

10

SUTTER'S FORT

October–November 1846
Steamboat Springs to Sutter's Fort

Ten days after the Paiute attack, the Harlan party caught up with the Boggs group. They met about seven miles from the Truckee River at a place called Steamboat Springs. Since it was already late in the afternoon, both wagon masters decided to stop for the night.

At dusk, Daniel sat with the Arnolds and Jim around the campfire. He drew his blankets tighter around his shoulders. The evening's chill paled in comparison to the coldness that caged his heart. He wasn't even aware of the falling snow until Dr. Arnold mentioned it.

"I do hope we won't run into a snowstorm." Dr. Arnold's clipped speech sounded even more British tonight. The elderly man sipped his steaming tea and then continued. "We experienced several severe snowstorms back in England the winter before we came to America. I cannot imagine being caught in one out here." Dr. Arnold glanced over at Jim who sat across from him smoking his pipe. "Do you think the wagon train will move on in the morning?"

Before Jim could answer, a ghastly wail pierced the air from the direction of Jim's wagon.

Daniel twisted the edges of his blanket between his hands. It sounded like Hannah's scream just after the arrow struck her chest.

Jim gazed at Dr. Arnold. With trembling hand, Jim plucked his pipe from between his lips. "No, Doctor, I don't believe we'll move on in the morning. I convinced both Boggs and Harlan to stay here one more day. Eliza's had severe stomach pains since yesterday."

Mrs. Arnold handed her teacup to her husband. "Oh, my. Why didn't you say something, Mr. Savage? I will check on the dear girl. Perhaps she has gone into labor."

Mrs. Arnold entered the Savage's wagon. Before long, she popped her head out the back. Strands of her silver hair, normally neatly pinned atop her head, escaped their restraint. "Daniel, dear. Please call on Mrs. Whittaker." Mrs. Arnold stopped to catch her breath. "She is much more experienced as a midwife than I am. We need her. Now."

Waiting for news of the impending birth, Daniel continued to sit with Jim and Dr. Arnold around the Savage's campfire. Other than Eliza's wails and the crush of stones as Jim paced from the wagon to the campfire, silence blanketed the night.

A few hours later, a baby's cry rang out.

Mrs. Arnold lifted the wagon's back flap. "It's a girl!"

Jim stopped pacing and removed the pipe from his mouth. "Is Eliza all right?" His voice cracked.

"Both she and your daughter are fine," Mrs. Arnold said. "You can see them now if you'd like."

Everyone took turns greeting Jim's new daughter and congratulating Eliza. Everyone, except Daniel. How could he be happy about a new life when his sister's had been so recently snuffed out? He continued to sit by the fire, unable to warm his insides, while Jim and the Arnolds chattered about their future plans in California.

After all the visitors had finally left, Daniel's eyelids began to droop.

Dr. Arnold stood and stretched. He turned to Mrs. Arnold. "Dear, I think we should retire for the evening. There doesn't seem to be anything else we can do here."

The doctor helped Mrs. Arnold stand. Before they turned to leave, Eliza stumbled out of her wagon. Her pallid face looked as white as her nightgown. No blanket draped her shoulders. A look of confusion filled her eyes.

"Get back into the wagon, dear girl," Mrs. Arnold scolded. "You'll catch your death of a cold out here."

"I just … I need … a little fresh air." Eliza's trembling voice sounded as weak as she looked. Her sweaty, dark brown hair, usually pulled back in a braid, now appeared wild and windswept as it fell to her shoulders in disarray. After a few moments, she cocooned herself again inside the wagon.

The next morning at breakfast Daniel asked about the baby's name.

"We offered a few suggestions." Mrs. Arnold handed him a plate of mush with bits of dried jerky, "but both

Jim and Eliza said they won't name the infant for at least another week."

Later that evening as Daniel prepared for bed, he glanced around the wagon's small interior. In one corner lay Hannah's doll. Why hadn't he gotten rid of it? Next to the doll sat the Arnold's Bible. He hadn't opened it since his sister died.

"Might as well toss that book into the fire, for all the good it's done me." He grabbed the Bible and tucked it under his arm. Opening the wagon's flaps, he readied himself to jump down. A wolf-like howl stopped him cold. The unearthly cry caused the blood to creep from his limbs. He tossed the Bible onto a pile of blankets inside the wagon, then joined the crowd gathering around the Savage's campfire.

"It's Jim," Dr. Arnold told Daniel.

From somewhere near the camp, another howl pierced the air.

Raising his eyebrows, Daniel glanced at Mrs. Arnold.

She sniffled, removed her spectacles, and dabbed her red-rimmed eyes with a handkerchief. "Eliza—" A sob choked off her words. "Eliza is dead."

For the first time, Daniel noticed the swathed bundle in Mrs. Arnold's arms. Jim's unnamed daughter. As if he'd swallowed a stone, his lungs refused to pull in a breath.

Mrs. Arnold handed the tiny package to Dr. Arnold. "Poor Eliza." Tears flowed down her wrinkled cheeks in crooked channels. "The woman never fully recovered from that mountain fever. I fear the strain of childbirth proved too much for her."

For the next few hours, Jim continued wailing from

somewhere outside the circle of wagons. Every cry tore at something inside of Daniel. Would the man stay out all night? What if animals attacked him? What if he never returned? By midnight, Daniel and several other men lit torches and went out to find him.

"Just bury me with my wife," Jim screamed as they dragged him back to camp. When someone finally suggested they give him what he asked, he stopped howling.

The next day, Daniel and a few others buried Eliza in a shallow grave. Jim placed his baby girl in the arms of Eliza's midwife, Mrs. Whittaker.

Daniel clambered into his wagon and brought out Hannah's doll. "The baby might like this when she gets a little older." He handed the doll to Mrs. Whittaker. "No sense in me keeping it." His heart contracted. "It was my sister's doll."

"I'm sure the baby will enjoy it." Mrs. Whittaker passed the doll to her husband as she juggled Jim's infant in the crook of her other arm. "Did your sister give the doll a name?"

Even though a light snow still fell to the ground, sweat beaded its way down Daniel's back. "Yes ma'am," he nodded. "She called it *Huhawira*. It means *moon* in the Ho-Chunk language."

Mrs. Whittaker wrinkled her nose. "Who-weer-u? Who-wa-hu? Can you repeat the name, please?"

Daniel shook his head. "Just tell her the doll's name is Sassafras."

"Oh, that's much easier." Mrs. Whittaker's smile didn't quite reach her eyes. "I'm sure she will enjoy it."

Jim gazed once more at his daughter. His face appeared to spasm in a wave of grief. Without a word, he saddled his favorite horse and clomped out of camp.

Daniel let his jaw drop. For a moment, time seemed to stop.

Jim's abandoning his little girl?

He's abandoning me?

Dr. Arnold patted Daniel's shoulder. "He'll be back. After all, he left his wagon here with all of his belongings. And, his spare horse."

The wagon train moved on. Jim's cousins took turns driving the man's wagon. For the next two days, Daniel kept a sharp lookout for Jim.

He never returned.

That evening, Daniel visited the Whittakers. Mrs. Whittaker rocked the baby as she sat on a log next to her husband near the family's campfire. A few feet away, a girl about ten giggled as she chased a younger boy around a wagon.

"Have you named the baby yet?" Daniel asked.

"I will when she's a bit stronger."

The baby's head poked out from beneath her blankets. Daniel moved closer and stroked the baby's tuft of brown hair. A tiny fist wriggled out of the bundle. He patted it. The back of her hand felt soft and silky. The baby unfurled her fingers and curled them around Daniel's thumb. Like the dam he'd once tried to build in the creek behind their house, he struggled to choke back a flood of emotions.

Poor baby girl. No Ma or Pa.

No family.

Just like me.

As he stumbled back to his wagon, Jim's cousin, Charles, approached. Jim's spare horse trailed behind him. "Peter and I decided you should have Jim's gelding." Charles offered Daniel the reins.

Daniel's throat burned as he stepped back and raised his hands, palms up. "I can't take Jim's horse."

"The man was your guardian. You at least deserve his horse." Charles kicked a rock with the toe of his boot. "I know he didn't leave you nothin' else. Besides. Peter and I have more'n enough to do, driving his wagon along with our own."

Several days later, Tom and Jacob arrived with supplies from Fort Sutter, raising everyone's spirits. Everyone's except his.

The next morning, Mrs. Arnold brought Daniel breakfast. He shook his head and held up a hand. "Please, Mrs. Arnold, you don't have to cook for me. I can fend for myself. You worked so hard caring for Eliza, and now you're helping with the baby. No need to care for me, too."

Mrs. Arnold continued to extend the tin plate full of venison and biscuits. Her tired blue eyes remained fixed on him. "We all need to keep up our health, young man. There'll be no argument about it."

Daniel nodded and accepted the plate. "Yes, ma'am."

Tears pooled in Mrs. Arnold's eyes. "Besides, I am no longer needed to help with Eliza's baby. Like her mother, that little girl wasn't strong enough for this harsh world. The good Lord saw fit to take her home last night."

His heart pushed against the walls of his chest. So much loss. Ma and Pa. Hannah. Morgan. Jim. Eliza. The baby. He couldn't take much more.

As the trail led higher through the Sierras and the air grew cooler, Daniel found it harder to breathe. The days blurred together into one. He'd outgrown his shoes, and his feet developed blisters. He focused on just putting one foot in front of the other.

When they stopped for the midday meal, he leaned against his wagon and removed his shoes. Tapping out several stones, he sighed. His shoes had developed holes where the soles had worn thin. Removing his socks, he wriggled his blistered toes. Without warning, a flood of emotions burst through the dam of his self-sufficiency. *What would Pa think of me now? I've lost Hannah. I've lost two guardians. At fourteen, I'm all alone in the world.*

A tear slid down his cheek. He'd been too busy surviving to even notice the passage of his birthday.

Later that evening, he tried on his father's boots—the ones he'd repaired for his pa's birthday the night of the house fire. Still too big. *Guess I still have a ways to go.*

The next morning when he rubbed his chin, bits of stubble pricked his fingers. He wagged his head. *I'm changing on the outside. But I doubt I'll ever be able to fill Pa's boots.*

That evening, the Arnolds invited Daniel to join them for supper. He turned them down. "I've still got plenty." He clenched and unclenched his jaw. As if his mouth were full of ash, he spit out the next words. "Remember, I'm only eating for one."

Sitting alone by his small campfire, questions consumed him. *What am I going to do when I reach California? How will I support myself? Where will I live?* Before he left Illinois, all he wanted was justice for his parents. Like the inside of his wagon without Hannah, that dream now seemed empty. Even if he did find those responsible for his parents' deaths, it wouldn't bring them back.

By November 5, Sutter's Fort lay only a day ahead. His spirit, like the soles of his shoes, had also worn thin.

"Jim is still your legal guardian," Dr. Arnold reminded Daniel as they neared the fort. "Perhaps he's waiting for you there."

Daniel didn't care. Once again, as when he first walked the trail with Virginia, people seemed more like mosquitoes than flowers. He waved a dismissive hand. "I'll ask when we get there, but I won't hold my breath."

When they arrived at the fort, Harlan ordered them to circle their wagons on the west side of the walled structure. When they finished, he stood atop a boulder inside the circle of wagons and called everyone together. "Mr. Sutter sent a messenger with instructions. He says most Injuns 'round these parts are friendly now, but it never hurts to take precautions. That's why he encouraged us to circle our wagons so we can keep the animals inside our enclosure."

The wagon master's pitch rose. "Also, Mr. Sutter's invited our company's leaders to meet with him inside the fort for supper tonight. He'll let us know how things are done 'round here so we can give you a full report in the morning. Tomorrow, we can all go inside to stock up on provisions.

Some of you may want to stay on at the fort for a spell. Mr. Sutter needs some skilled workers to help with his enterprise here."

As Harlan stepped down from the boulder, Dr. Arnold and Mrs. Arnold approached him. Daniel trailed behind them.

"I noticed the American flag waving above the fort," Dr. Arnold said. "I thought Mr. Sutter and his fort were under the authority of the Mexican government, not the United States. Why isn't he flying the Mexican flag?"

Raising an eyebrow, the wagon master nodded. "I wondered that too. Sutter's messenger informed me that, back in April, Mexican cavalry attacked a group of U.S. soldiers between the Rio Grande and Nueces Rivers. It's an area we've claimed as part of the United States, but Mexico says it belongs to them. In July, Commodore Sloat sailed into the port of Monterey, read a proclamation of war between us and Mexico, and raised the American flag. Sutter's messenger told me we're still at war with Mexico, but the U.S. claims California now belongs to the United States."

"My." Dr. Arnold glanced at Daniel. "Much has happened since we left Illinois."

"The messenger also gave me something for you." Harlan handed Dr. Arnold a note.

"What is it, dear?" Mrs. Arnold laid a hand on her husband's arm.

The doctor unfolded the note, scanned it, and gazed at his wife. "Mr. Sutter has also invited you and me to supper tonight." The doctor turned his attention back to the wagon master. "Do you know why Mr. Sutter included us on his guest list? How did he even know we were part of this wagon train?"

Harlan offered a half-smile. "Guess you've got me to blame for that. Mr. Sutter's messenger asked if you were part of our company. When I told him you were, he said Sutter met your brother a few months ago when he did some business with the Hudson Bay Company. Your brother asked Sutter to be on the lookout for you. It seems Sutter has a package to pass on to you from your brother. Mr. Sutter will give it to you after supper tonight."

When Harlan left, the doctor showed Daniel and Mrs. Arnold the evening's menu listed on the invitation. The meal would include beefsteaks, potatoes, green beans, and fresh bread. Daniel's mouth watered.

Mrs. Arnold took off her spectacles, wiped them on the edge of her apron, and looked up at her husband. "If it is all right with you, dear, perhaps Daniel could accompany you to the dinner this evening. I am so weary from our long journey. I would rather retire early tonight."

Perhaps Mrs. Arnold really was too tired to attend the affair. Or maybe she thought a hearty meal would cheer him up. Either way, Daniel was grateful for the opportunity to eat food that he didn't have to kill, skin, or cook for himself.

During the dinner, Daniel savored every bite of his juicy steak. Unlike most of the food on the trail, this meal didn't have any pebbles or dirt or ash in it. While others talked about possible jobs at the fort, or signing up to fight the Mexicans, Daniel focused on grabbing another piece of the thick warm bread before the plate passed him by. Snagging a slice, he slathered it with creamy butter as Sutter bragged about his enterprise.

Sutter stroked his long, dark brown mustache. "You

probably couldn't see our livestock from the west side of the fort, but we currently have 3,500 head of cattle, 3,000 sheep, 1,700 horses and mules, and 1,000 hogs. California is certainly a land of opportunity."

"But doesn't California belong to the Mexicans?" one of the men in Harlan's group asked. "To own land here, don't we have to become Mexican citizens first?"

Sutter cleared his throat. "Most around here address me as *Captain* Sutter. I served in the Swiss army while a citizen in Switzerland before I emigrated to the United States."

The man's face reddened.

"But to answer your question," Captain Sutter continued, "Yes, that will soon change. The United States is currently at war with Mexico. Honestly, if the United States hadn't gone to war with Mexico over these western lands, most likely Great Britain or another European power would have tried to take over. Ever since Mexico gained its independence from Spain twenty years ago, its government has been marked by instability and corruption. Do you know, over the last twenty years, Mexico has appointed at least fourteen different governors to California?"

The men continued to talk about politics. Daniel, for his part, focused on the yeasty aroma of the fresh bread, the tangy fragrance of the sliced oranges encircling the plate of beans, the fruity, heady, bouquet emanating the men's wine glasses.

"Hey." A bearded man sitting next to Daniel nudged his arm. "Aren't you that young blacksmith a travelin' with Jim Savage and his wife?"

Daniel swallowed his bite of potatoes. "Yes, sir. Were you part of Boggs' wagon train? You don't look familiar."

"I was," the man nodded. "Heard about Savage abandoning you after his wife died. Sad story, what happened to the wife and baby. One of Sutter's men said Savage and a few other pioneers rode in here a couple of weeks ago and immediately volunteered to fight the Mexicans. Heard it pays seven dollars a month if you join up."

A man sitting across from Daniel snapped his head up and whistled. "You say fighting to make California part of U.S. pay seven dollar a month? I come to America five year ago. I come from Prussia. No job. Now in California. Still no job. Maybe I sign up."

Sutter stopped talking with Mr. Boggs and peered at the Prussian. "Fighting as a volunteer in our war with Mexico is one job opportunity," he said in a loud voice.

Everyone stopped talking.

Sutter sipped his wine. "I also need skilled workers here at the fort. I'm looking for a trained carpenter, another cooper, a blacksmith, and a miller. If you're interested, speak with my assistant in the morning after the workers go out to the fields."

"This is quite an establishment you've built here," Mr. Harlan said, scooping up another spoonful of vegetables. "We're mighty grateful for the supplies you sent our way when we were still on the east side of the Sierras." The wagon master lifted his glass of wine. "I propose a toast."

Daniel raised his water glass.

"Hear, hear," Mr. Boggs said, also raising his glass. "We pioneers are mighty grateful for your generosity, Captain Sutter. I heard you sent supplies with James Reed a few weeks ago to help rescue his family and the others in the Donner Party who are trapped in the Sierra snows."

Virginia? Daniel's hand jerked. Water sloshed out of his glass and onto the white linen tablecloth. He quickly grabbed his napkin to dab the spill.

Sutter raised his eyebrows at Daniel. He then nodded his head toward Mr. Boggs, acknowledging his toast. "I do what I can. Sad story about Mr. Reed, though. He and a few men tried to get supplies up to the trapped pioneers, but the deep snows forced them to turn back. Those poor souls will have to make the best of their situation until it's easier to get through. Unfortunately, that will probably take a few months until the weather warms up. In the meantime, I heard Reed volunteered to help fight the Mexicans."

Daniel couldn't focus on the rest of the conversation. Only one thought filled his head. *Would he ever see Virginia again?*

S.T.E.A.M.

Finish students' Final Project at:
https://drive.google.com/file/d/1I0beEy-GFa-JmV01bc_bfebhrdMv9bF0C/view?usp=sharing

11

FAMILY

November–December 1846
Sutter's Fort to Yerba Buena

The next morning when Daniel toured Sutter's Fort, he spied a large group of Indians near the well. Clothed only in breechcloths, the men sat on the ground next to a hollowed-out tree trunk. Curious, Daniel peered into the trough. Inside pooled what looked like a thin porridge. He wrinkled his nose. *Must be their breakfast.*

The Indians eagerly scooped out the gruel with their hands. A few minutes later, they picked up their sickles and rakes and headed out the front gate.

Daniel shook his head. *Couldn't Sutter at least give them bowls?*

Walking past a row of stalls on his left, Daniel passed a cooperage and a gun shop. Hearing the bell-like clang of a hammer against a horseshoe, he followed the sound, determined to find the smithy and ask if he needed an apprentice. Before he reached the shop, a familiar voice drew his attention.

Glancing to his right, he saw Matthew Brody and his brother, Josiah, standing with other pioneers out in the courtyard. A middle-aged man stood at a wooden podium in front of them. He recognized the man as Mr. Hastings—the man who'd encouraged them to take the shortcut that wasn't really a shortcut.

"Captain Hastings," Matthew called out. "I heard tell we can earn seven dollars a month if we sign up to fight. That true?"

Hastings tucked his red flannel shirt more firmly into his gray woolen pants. "It's true, son. We're forming a volunteer unit that'll ride out from here in two days. You'll join up with Captain Frémont's battalion in Monterey." The man dipped his pen in an inkwell and pointed to the paper in front of him. "If you're at least seventeen and you want to join, print your name here, then sign next to it."

He knew Matthew was seventeen, but not Josiah. And yet, they both eagerly signed the paper.

Daniel snickered. *Good thing Matthew and Josiah stayed in school long enough to learn how to write their names.* He pinched his lower lip between his teeth. He could also probably pass for seventeen, but he had no desire to join a war, especially if it meant fighting alongside Jim or the Brody brothers. He continued on to the blacksmith shop to ask about an apprenticeship.

"Sorry, son. I need a full-fledged blacksmith. No time to take on an apprentice." The large bearded man stood in front of Daniel and wiped his sooty hands on his blackened apron. "I 'specially need someone trained as a saddler. But I wish you luck." The blacksmith shook Daniel's hand and returned to hammering a horseshoe.

As if a ball of iron had lodged in his lungs, Daniel found it hard to breathe. His stomach spasmed. Sweat prickled his neck and dribbled down his back. Maybe he could sell his wagon and buy enough supplies to ride to San José and apprentice with a blacksmith there. It seemed like a long shot, but what other choice did he have?

That afternoon as he walked back to his wagon, he passed the Brody brothers sitting on a log, drinking from whiskey bottles.

"Come join, us Daniel," Mr. Brody called out. "We're celebratin' our safe arrival."

Daniel clenched his jaw. A dark cloud slipped past the sun and over his heart. "Not all of us arrived safely."

"Come now, boy." Mr. Brody waved his bottle. "I've promised my boys this is the last drop I'll drink till their safe return from the war. Did ya hear they signed up to join Frémont's Battalion today?"

Daniel glanced at Matthew. The miscreant gave him a suit-yourself-shrug.

Back at his wagon, Daniel sat on a large boulder eating a plate of beans. Dr. Arnold approached carrying a small leather pouch.

"Mrs. Arnold and I leave tomorrow for Yerba Buena." The elderly man sat next to Daniel on the boulder. "Have you decided what you're going to do?"

"Might go to Pueblo San José and look for a job," he said around a mouthful of beans.

The doctor nodded. "That's one idea." He jangled the pouch between his hands. "Mr. Sutter gave me this bag last night after supper. It appears my brother left me some money to assist in our travel from here to Yerba Buena.

He says the house he's purchased for us has a beautiful view of the bay. Yerba Buena is a small settlement of about 450 people, but my brother predicts it will explode into a booming city once the war with Mexico is over."

Daniel shoveled another spoonful of beans into his mouth. "Sounds like a good plan."

"Yerba Buena is a better port for commerce than Monterey," the doctor continued. "My brother believes ships from as far away as China and the Hawaiian Islands will dock there to do business."

"I'm happy you'll be with family again, Dr. Arnold." Daniel pushed the last spoonful of beans around his plate without scooping them up. His side ached as he chewed on the word "family"—something he'd lost and would never get back.

Looking off into the distance, Dr. Arnold jostled his bag once more. "I've been told the journey to Yerba Buena is another ninety miles west. Mrs. Arnold is worried it might be a difficult journey for just the two of us. We plan to trade in our oxen for horses and hire someone to drive our wagon while we follow along on horseback. Mrs. Arnold suggested I ask if you would be interested in driving our wagon. We would pay you, of course."

Daniel stared at his last spoonful of beans and, once again, considered his options. He could join the volunteer army fighting for control of California. He could ride to San José in hopes of finding a job as a blacksmith's apprentice. Or, he could help the Arnolds get to Yerba Buena and perhaps find a job there. At least he'd be with people he knew.

"I know we're not family," the doctor added as he turned

to face Daniel. "But what is family, anyway? Isn't it the place where you find love and security? Where you're accepted for who you are and supported to become all you were meant to be?"

Daniel allowed his gaze to meet the doctor's. He squeezed his hands tight as a flame sparked in his chest.

"Truth be told," the elderly gentleman continued, "Mrs. Arnold and I have felt that way about you and Hannah ever since we met you." He let the bag rest in his lap as he removed his spectacles and cleaned them with a handkerchief. "God has allowed you to go through so much, Daniel. Perhaps it's time for you to find a place of rest, at least for a while, until you get your feet under you and discover what is your next adventure." He returned his glasses to his face.

Daniel's spark of heat flickered, flared, and flamed from chest to his limbs. With wide eyes, he stared at the elderly man. "Exactly what are you saying, doctor?"

"I'm saying Mrs. Arnold and I would like you to become part of our family. Perhaps not officially, but for all intents and purposes—family. We're inviting you to come live with us in Yerba Buena. You're only thirteen, correct?"

"Fourteen, sir, since the end of July."

"Fourteen." Dr. Arnold nodded. "Perhaps you can find a job in Yerba Buena once you settle in. See where life takes you. We'd like to be part of your life as you prepare for your next journey."

Wasn't that what he wanted all along? He thought searching for justice, even revenge, for his parents' deaths would fill the hole their absence left. It didn't. Pastor Lovejoy's words echoed in his mind. *If you seek justice on your own terms, the anger will eat you up until there's nothing left of you.*

Daniel stared at his fisted hands and slowly opened them. He still wanted justice for his parents, but not at the expense of shutting everyone out of his life. He was finally ready to start living again. To start living with a family again.

"Yes, sir." Daniel let a small smile tug at his lips. "I'd like to have you be part of my new journey. My new family. I'd like that very much."

S.T.E.A.M.

Complete students' Final Project at:
https://www.mariesontag.com/resources/teacher/

DISCUSSION QUESTIONS

1. In Chapter 1, Daniel says, *I thought life was supposed to be fair. Ma and Pa always put others first. How could God let someone get away with murdering them?* Do you think life is supposed to be fair? Why or why not?

2. Who do you think experienced the most "fair" life in the story. Explain why you think this.

3. What do you think of Jim in the beginning of the story? Does your impression of him change by the end of the book? Why or why not?

4. How does Hannah change throughout the story? What happens to bring about these changes?

5. Describe Daniel's biggest strength and weakness. How do these impact him and his decisions throughout the story?

6. How did Daniel feel about the Kaw Indians he saw on the Great Plains? (See Chapter 5). Why do you think he felt this way?

7. Most pioneers believed they had a right to cross the Great Plains and the Unorganized Territory, killing animals for food along the way. Do you agree? Why or why not?

8. An ancient Greek philosopher, Plato, once had an argument with a man named Thrasymachus. We can just call him Mr. T. Mr. T believed that the strongest people in a society get to decide what is just and what is not. Put another way, we could say that Mr. T believed, "Might makes right." Another famous person, President Lincoln, once said that doing the right thing is what makes you strong. Lincoln's exact quote was, "Let us have faith that right makes might, and in that faith, let us, to the end, dare to do our duty as we understand it." (February 26, 1860, Cooper Union Address). What do you think is the difference between these two statements—*Might Makes Right*, and *Right Makes Might*?

9. After Number 9 in the column below, place a check-mark beneath the phrase you agree with the most, "Might Makes Right," or "Right Makes Might." On a separate piece of paper for 9, explain why you agree with this phrase.

Might Makes Right	Right Make Might
9.	
10.	
11.	
12.	

10. See https://kids.kiddle.co/United_States_Declaration_of_Independence and scroll down to the section titled "Simple English Translation." After reading this, check the column above next to Number 10 to indicate what, in your opinion, the writers of the U.S. Declaration believed: "Might Makes Right," or "Right Makes Might?" On your separate piece of paper, labeling it 10, provide evidence to back up your opinion.

11. On the above column next to Number 11, check which phrase you think Daniel would have agreed with the most. On your separate piece of paper next to Number 11 explain why you think this.

12. Which phrase best shows what many American leaders may have believed when it came to the treatment of the Native Americans in the 1800s? Mark it on the chart above. Why do you think this? Explain it as Number 12 on your separate piece of paper.

CAST OF CHARACTERS

in California Trail Discovered

Sequential Order

Daniel Whitcomb—A thirteen-year-old fictional character from Princeton Township, Illinois, Daniel works as a blacksmith apprentice under Morgan Savage's tutorship. Later, Morgan's older brother, Jim Savage, becomes his guardian when Morgan marries Frances Brisbin on the Oregon Trail.

Morgan Savage—A twenty-one-year-old historical figure and younger brother of Jim Savage, Morgan is (fictionally) a business partner with Daniel's father in the blacksmithing business. When Daniel's parents die, Morgan (fictionally) becomes Daniel and Hannah's guardian.

Hannah Whitcomb—A fictional ten-year-old stepsister of Daniel who once lived with Indians after her father died.

Pastor Owen Lovejoy—A thirty-five-year-old historical character who pastors the Hampshire Colony Congregational Church in Princeton, Illinois. His home is an important station along the Underground Railroad.

James (Jim) Savage—A twenty-nine-year-old historical character and older brother of Morgan Savage. Jim, along with his wife Eliza, his brother Morgan, and several cousins travel on a wagon train led by William Russell in 1846. At first, Jim plans to go with his family to the Oregon Country, but changes his mind on the way and decides to go to California. Fictionally, he serves as Daniel and Hannah Whitcomb's guardian after his brother (in real life) marries Frances Brisbin when the wagon train nears Ft. Laramie.

Frances Brisbin—An eighteen-year-old historical character traveling with her father and brothers to the Oregon Country. She marries Morgan Savage while on the trail.

Colonel William Russell—A forty-four-year-old historical character who is the leader of the 1846 wagon train that includes members of the Donner Party, the Savages, and the Brisbins. He, along with several others, leave the wagon train when they near Ft. Laramie to travel to California by mule.

Lilburn W. Boggs—A former governor of Missouri, the fifty-year-old historical character is a member of Daniel's wagon train in 1846. He is married to Panthea Grant Boone, a granddaughter of Daniel Boone. When they near Ft. Laramie, Colonel Russell leaves the wagon train and Boggs becomes the wagon master.

Lewis Keseberg—He is a thirty-two-year-old German immigrant. A historical character and one of the Donner Party members, he resorts to cannibalism while trapped in the Sierra Nevada snows with other members of the Donner-Reed group.

James Reed—A forty-six-year-old historical character from Springfield, Illinois, he and his family are members of the Donner Party traveling with the Russell wagon train. When those in his wagon train decide to take the Greenwood Cutoff, the Donner-Reed group chooses to continue south and take the Hastings Cutoff to meet up with the California Trail. Jim Savage goes with them, hoping to reach California sooner than the others. James Reed and his family are among the few who survive the winter in the Sierras.

Virginia Reed—A historical character, Virginia is the 12-year-old stepdaughter of James Reed. She becomes a friend of the fictional characters Daniel and Hannah on the wagon train.

Patty Reed—A historical character, Patty is the younger sister of Virginia Reed.

Matthew and Josiah Brody—They are fictional characters from Princeton Township, Illinois and neighbors of Daniel Whitcomb. Matthew, seventeen, and his younger brother Josiah start fights with Daniel. Matthew and Josiah's father drinks too much and usually leaves his sons to care for themselves.

John Breen—An Irish fourteen-year-old historical character who is part of the Donner Party, he befriends Daniel while on the wagon train.

Dr. George Arnold and his wife Caroline Arnold—Fictional characters, Dr. Arnold is an eye doctor who helps Hannah with her eye problem. He and his wife befriend Daniel and Hannah. Originally from England, the Arnolds travel with the wagon train to California where they plan to meet up with the doctor's brother in Yerba Buena (San Francisco).

James Clyman—A historical character, he was a mountain man who also traveled with Jedediah Smith. He meets up with the Russell/Boggs wagon train at Ft. Laramie. He tries to dissuade them from taking the Hastings Cutoff.

Lansford Hastings—Trained as a lawyer, this historical character wrote *The Emigrants' Guide to Oregon and California* at the age of twenty-six. Through this book, he hopes to encourage Americans to move West. He hopes that, by flooding California with emigrants, it will become the Republic of California, similar to the way Texas broke away from Mexico and became a republic. He hopes to gain a high office in this new republic. The shortcut to California he mentions in his book becomes known as the "Hastings Cutoff." However, Hastings never took this cutoff himself before writing his book. He isn't aware that his so-called "cutoff" is more difficult to travel than the Greenwood Cutoff most other travelers took to reach the California Trail.

Tamsen Donner—A historical character, Mrs. Donner was an intelligent woman, proficient in mathematics, geometry, and philosophy. She was fluent in French, an avid botanist, a competent painter, and a writer of prose and poetry. She promised the editor of the *Springfield Journal* that she'd send him accounts of their journey West whenever she was able. While at Beaver Creek, she sent an article to the editor by way of a mountain man who was traveling back to the states. She was married to George Donner, the leader of the Donner-Reed Party. Her party separated from the Boggs' wagon train to take the Hastings Cutoff, hoping to reach California faster than the rest of the Boggs' group. At the age of forty-five, she and her family were trapped in the Sierra Nevada snows where half of their group died from exposure or starvation, including Mr. and Mrs. Donner.

George Harlan—This forty-four-year-old historical figure and the group of people he leads reach Ft. Bridger at about the same time as Daniel and Jim Savage's group. Daniel and Jim, along with the Donner-Reed Party, separate from Boggs' wagon train at the Greenwood Cutoff. Later, however, the Donner-Reed pioneers fall behind Daniel's group, and Jim decides not to wait for the Donner-Reed group to catch up. Jim's wagon train leaves Ft. Bridger with the Harlan pioneers. After leaving Ft.

Bridger, Harlan's wagon train travels through Hastings Cutoff before the Donner Party reaches this so-called "shortcut," enabling those led by Harlan to escape the Sierra snows that trap the Donner Party for the winter.

John Sutter—A historical character, Sutter arrived in New York in 1834 after leaving his wife and four children in Switzerland. After moving to California, which was controlled by Mexico, he became a Mexican citizen, allowing him to obtain a land grant from the Mexican governor, Alvarado. Alvarado employed him as a Justice of the Peace, providing him with the civil authority to administrate justice on the Sacramento Frontier. Sutter named his settlement New Switzerland (Nueva Helvecia). Bordered by the Feather and Sacramento rivers, his property consisted of almost 48,000 acres. By the time Daniel and those in the Harlan party reached Sutter's Fort, Sutter had a farming operation that grew wheat, barley, peas, beans, and cotton with the help of Native Americans. He hired tradesmen from all nations and created businesses on his property that developed furs, whiskey, brandy distilling and beer brewing, and even exported wheat to Russian Alaska. In addition, his ranch had 1,700 horses and mules, 4,000 cattle, and 3,000 sheep. He trained fifty Native Americans as his home guard, dressing them in military uniforms and furnishing them with muskets. He also maintained a white military force of over twenty men. For defense, the fort maintained twenty-four canons and other smaller artillery pieces. Sutter provided free shelter and supplies to weary settlers, and helped rescue the stranded Donner

Party of pioneers in 1846 and 1847. He even created a booklet he had published in Germany, advertising for settlers to come join him at the fort. The American Army took over the fort in the Mexican-American War of 1846-1847.

CAST OF CHARACTERS

in California Trail Discovered

Alphabetical Order by Last Name

George and Caroline Arnold
Lilburn W. Boggs
John Breen
Frances Brisbin
Matthew and Josiah Brody
James Clyman
Tamsen Donner
George Harlan
Lansford Hastings
Lewis Keseberg
Pastor Owen Lovejoy
James Reed
Patty Reed
Virginia Reed
Colonel William Russell
James (Jim) Savage

Morgan Savage
John Sutter
Daniel Whitcomb
Hannah Whitcomb

AUTHOR'S NOTE

Dear Reader,

Thank you! Thank you, dear reader, for giving your time to read this book. It means a lot that you trusted me to entertain, and hopefully excite, you with this story. Stories need an audience and I appreciate you being my audience for just a little while. So, once again, thank you.

Now I have a request. I want as many readers as possible to discover the story of Daniel and his family and friends, and your voice can help do that. Please consider leaving a review on your favorite social media platform or book-seller's website. And tell a friend! Word-of-mouth is the best way to introduce this story to other readers.

I would love to hear from you. Feel free to email me at mariesontag@mariesontag.com or post on my Facebook page.

ABOUT THE AUTHOR

Formerly from California, Dr. Marie Sontag resides in Texas with her husband, moving there to be closer to their grandchildren, the light of their lives. She taught middle school for over fifteen years, is a member of ACFW and SCBWI, and still dreams lesson plans in her head at night! With a BA in social science, and an MA and PhD in education, she loves to bring the past to life for middle grade and young adult readers (as well as adults). For more information about her and her books or to schedule a school visit or writer's workshop visit her online at:

https://www.mariesontag.com/contact/